FANTASY ADVENTURES 9

Books edited by Philip Harbottle

Books edited by Philip Harbottle & Sean Wallace

FANTASY ADVENTURES 9

EDITED BY PHILIP HARBOTTLE

COSMOS

FANTASY ADVENTURES 9

Cosmos Books / Wildside Press
P.O. Box 301, Holicong, PA 18928-0301
www.wildsidepress.com
www.cosmos-books.com

WORLD FIRST EDITION

10 9 8 7 6 5 4 3 2 1

ISBN: 1-59224-216-2

CONTENTS

SPAWN OF JUPITER

E. C. Tubb

Durgan heard the sound as he crested the rise and he froze, eyes narrowed as he probed the dimness. Dimness, not dark, for it was never dark at night on Ganymede, the great ball of Jupiter filling the sky took care of that, the flaring mystery of the Red Spot seeming to look down like a watchful eye.

The sound came again, a stirring, a scuffle as of a boot against vegetation, a movement of bulk. Durgan stepped from the path into the shadow of a clump of *leetha* bushes

Carefully he eased the bulging pack from his shoulders and rested it quietly on the ground. Picking up a handful of stones he threw one far down the trail in the direction from which he had come.

"Listen!" The voice was a whisper. "Did you hear that?"

Durgan threw another stone.

"Someone's coming. Get ready!"

Two of them at least but it was unlikely there would be more. Two men were enough to handle an unsuspecting harvester and more would only lessen the individual share.

They would be waiting on either side of the path, one lower down than the other, and would attack from both front and rear. If merciful they might not actually kill him, simply knock him unconscious and strip him of everything of value, but, to be naked on Ganymede, was to be dead.

Durgan crept silently through the bushes, easing aside the lacey fronds and letting them spring back with a minimum of noise. A stone turned beneath his boot and he almost fell, recovering his balance with a rustle of leaves He sprang forward as a shape loomed suddenly upright turning with a glimmer of whiteness from the face, a brighter shine from the upraised knife.

Durgan met the threat of the blade with a thrust of his own, the knife whipping from the top of his boot and lancing forward all in one smooth motion. The point hit the exposed column of the throat, ripped into flesh and muscle, cutting the great arteries and releasing a fountain of blood.

Dying the man fell, threshing, ugly sounds coming from his throat.

"Jarl?"

Durgan reached for his gun as the other man called from the shadowed dimness.

"Jarl?"

Durgan fired, the gout of flame traversing the path impinging on the upright figure, searing and penetrating with a shaft of irresistible heat. The man screamed, his body a flaring pillar of fire as leatheroid crisped and burned, falling with an odor of charred meat, his chest and lungs totally destroyed.

For five minutes Durgan waited, crouched in the shadows beside the path, gun steady in his hand as his eyes searched the night. Then he holstered the weapon and looked at the first man he had killed.

He was young with the facial attributes of a wolf, teeth bared and snarling even in death. His clothing was filthy, his boots worn, black crescents beneath his nails. He had no gun, no pack, only the knife and a thick club. His companion was much the same. Two scavengers who had sought one victim too many.

Returning to the clump of *leethan* bushes Durgan picked up his pack, shouldered it, continued on his way.

An hour later he reached Candara.

The settlement was a ramshackle place, a maze of buildings, shacks, hovels built of stone and dirt, looming warehouses and plastic constructions. The streets were unpaved, thick with litter and filth, rutted and splotched with odorous puddles. To one side the landing field rested beneath a continuous haze of light, the tall contours of the control tower spidery against the glowing disc of Jupiter.

As he hit the edge of the settlement a *rykat* barked a warning, the sharp, thin sound eerie in its haunting loneliness. A window slammed and a man called out.

"I've got a gun. Try anything and I'll shoot!"

Durgan walked past, silent, hearing the *rykat* bark again, the man's muttered cursing and the slam of the closing window. Deeper into the maze of buildings he heard the sound of music and laughter, the rattle of glasses, the unmistakable whirling noise made by a spinning wheel. Keeping to the center of the path, his hand resting on the butt of his holstered gun, he made his way to where a tall building rested on the edge of the landing field.

"You're late." The factor, a thin-faced man with red-rimmed eyes and a thin, predatory nose, glared from behind his counter as Durgan entered the trading post. "I was just about to call it a day. Can't it wait?"

For answer Durgan dropped the pack from his shoulders and lifted it to the counter. Opening it he produced a transparent plastic bag filled with grayish pods each two inches long and a quarter wide. Raw *kalsh*, the vegetable compound which, when cleaned and refined, would fetch twice its weight in gold when sold on Earth.

The factor pursed his lips in a soundless whistle.

"Man! That's some harvest! How long have you been out?"

"Six weeks." Durgan was curt. "I want to check it in. Weigh it, seal it, and give me a receipt. We can finish the deal later."

"Why not now?"

"Just do as I say."

Durgan leaned against the counter as the factor busied himself with scales and seals. The overhead light illuminated the strong lines of his face, the tall length of his body. It was a hard face and a muscular body both blurred a little now by fatigue, the eyes creped with tiny lines, the shoulders a trifle bowed. Six weeks in the Freelands was a long time for any one man to harvest.

"You want some spending money?" The factor came to the counter, papers in his hands. "A couple of hundred, say?"

Durgan nodded.

"I thought so. Just sign here and put your thumb here." The factor watched as Durgan followed instructions. "You know the old saying? Work hard and play hard? If you want some fun Madam Kei's got some new talent just arrived."

"No thanks," said Durgan.

"Each to his own poison," said the factor. He reached out and touched a spot on Durgan's tunic, frowning as he examined the carmine stain on his finger. "You have any trouble?"

"Should I have had?"

"You know better than me, mister. I just buy the stuff. Here's your cash. Drop in tomorrow and we can finish the deal." He looked at Durgan's extended hand. "Something else?"

"The receipt."

"Oh! Sure! I forgot." The factor handed it over, looking at the name. "Hey! There's something else slipped my mind. A dame's been asking for you. Said she'd wait in the *Purple Puppy*. You know it?"

"I know it. What did she want?"

The factor shrugged. "That she didn't say."

Durgan saw the woman the moment he stepped into the tavern. She sat alone at a table close to the stage, long legged, dressed in clean leatheroid, high boots, pants, blouse and tunic. A holstered gun lay flat against her stomach. Blonde hair was pulled back from her face in a pony tail which rested on her left shoulder. Her face was round, full-lipped, with a determined jaw and eyes. She was a woman but there was nothing soft about her as there was nothing soft about Ganymede. She was, he guessed, about twenty-five which made her five years younger than himself.

To the bartender he said, "Give me a bottle of *zulack* and a couple of glasses." Paying he added, "The woman facing the stage. Who is she?"

The man shrugged. "A drifter. Came in here about three weeks ago. Some of the boys tried their hand but she soon made the position clear. One of them wouldn't learn so she burnt a hole in his stomach. No one's bothered her since then."

Durgan nodded, picked up his bottle and glasses and headed towards where she sat, halting at a table at her side. As he sat the floor show commenced and he opened the bottle, threw away the top inch of liquor and filled one of the glasses. Sipping he watched the performance.

Someone had imported a troupe of dancers, sleek, olive-skinned women with long, black hair and flounced skirts, who stamped and pirouetted to the blood-stirring rattle of castanets. Behind them a man lifted his voice in the undulating wail of a flamenco as his fingers danced over the strings of a guitar.

It was an odd troupe to be found in such a place for little of the Inner Worlds touched the Outer Planets and Ganymede was used to cruder entertainment. *Wejack* birds, clipped and fitted with iron spurs, set to fight against each other to the death, broken singers on the last lap of their careers, jugglers, acrobats, mutants who swallowed fire, men who fought with spiked gloves to the screamed encouragement of their backers. These brought a touch of Earth, of sun and sea and shining beaches, of grapes and scented air, of rainbows and gentle breezes.

One day, perhaps, he would see it again. One day.

He drank the *zulack* and refilled his glass. A hand caught his own as he made to set down the bottle.

"You have two glasses," said the woman. "Would one be for me?"

"It might."

"Meaning that you are uncharitable?"

"Meaning that I would rather not drink with strangers." He met the coolness of the blue eyes. "Perhaps we should introduce ourselves."

"You are Brad Durgan," she said. "I am Sheila Moray. Now may I join you?"

He nodded, pouring the second glass full as she took a chair, handing it to her, suddenly acutely aware of her femininity, the sensuous throb of the music.

"I've been waiting for you," she said. "But, of course, you know that. The factor would have told you."

"He told me that a woman wanted to see me. He didn't say who and he didn't say why." Durgan drank more of the *zulack*. It was a hundred proof spirit, flavored with *kalsh*-pods, a limpid green devil containing smoldering fires.

They burned away some of his fatigue and a few of his memories. The scent of charred flesh, of newly shed blood, of straining weeks of constant anxiety, of fear and failure, of a future which held no hope and little promise.

"You drink too much," she said as he refilled his glass. "Or shouldn't I say that?"

"You shouldn't."

"Then let's talk of something else. Of the dancers, perhaps. You like them?"

"They're different."

"They were heading for Callisto, on contract to the Ku Fung franchise, but their ship developed a split tube lining and they docked here for repairs."

"So?"

"Callisto. Twice as far from Jupiter as we are now. A satellite almost the twin of Ganymede. You know about Callisto?"

"I know."

"And Amalthea?"

"A small world, a hundred miles in diameter, a hundred and thirteen thousand miles from the center of Jupiter." His hand tightened around his glass. "I know Amalthea."

"Yes," she said quietly. "You would. It's the bucket boat depot. Right?"

He swallowed the *zulack* in a single gulp, refilling the glass as the dancers came to the end of their performance.

Men rose, shouting, flinging a shower of coins on the stage.

One, bolder than the rest, sprang on the platform, his hands grabbing at a woman. He caught the shoulder-strap of her flounced gown, olive-skin glowing in the light as he ripped at the material. From the wings ran two men, hard-faced, armed. They clubbed down the intruder and stood, hands on guns, as the dancers left the stage.

They were replaced by a weary comedian who thickened the air with the blueness of his painful jokes.

"They clubbed the wrong man," said Sheila dispassionately. "That creep should be put in a sack and left as bait for gizzards."

"He's doing his best," said Durgan. "We all do our best."

"And where does it get you? Home? Earth? Back to comfort and safety? How long does a man have to harvest before he hits the jackpot?" She reached forward and rested her hand on his own. It was slender, the skin smooth and uncalloused, the nails reflecting the light with a pearly sheen. "There's blood on your tunic. This time you won, the next, who knows? Is that how you want to end? Meat for the scavengers?"

He met her eyes. "You're saying something, but what? And why are you interested in me? I've never seen you before."

"That's true."

"Then why the interest?"

"You're tall," she said. "Tough, a good-looker. For most girls that would be reason enough. But they would want something. I don't. Instead I can offer you the biggest thing you've ever met in your life. A chance at the jackpot. Money enough to set you up on Earth, a farm on Mars, a dome on Venus—you name it and it's yours."

Durgan was ironic. "Sure—and all I have to do is to give you a stake so you can go and collect the lost treasure of Ma Kalah. Bury it, girl! You're talking to the wrong man!"

"And you're jumping to conclusions." Her hand lifted, caught his wrist as he lifted the glass, twisted so that the *zulack* fell in a glinting stream to the surface of the table. "What are you, a sponge? Has that stuff rotted your mind and blocked your ears? I'm talking, Brad, can't you even listen?"

"To what?"

"A proposition. A trip to Callisto all expenses paid and a bonus for wasted time if you turn down the offer."

"And that is?"

"I don't know." Her eyes were frank. "I was sent to collect you and that's all. But it's something big, that at least I know. Agree and we can leave within the hour."

Durgan shook his head.

"You're turning me down?"

"No," he said. "But we can't leave until tomorrow. I've got money owing and I want to collect."

Distances were relatively unimportant in the Jovian system, only time was of value. Time to skirt the mammoth globe of the primary, to edge along the trap of its gravity well, to juggle speed and direction so as to reach where you wanted to go. Other things were minor but ever-present hazards, the threat of solar flares, trapped debris that added to the multiple moons, wandering fragments of interstellar rubbish which had been snared by the giant planet.

Durgan slept the major part of the journey, waking hours before landing, joining the girl in the compact lounge of the inter-moon transport. She had changed and now wore a short dress of glittering fiber, matching boots riding high on her thighs, a belt of synthetic gems accentuating the swell of her hips. Her hair, groomed and curled, hung like a curtain of shimmering gold on the rounded smoothness of her shoulders. To his questions she said, "Wait. You'll get all the answers after we land."

Callisto wasn't Ganymede though both had much the me mass and bulk. Here the big companies had established their franchises, terraforming the globe with imbedded devices, setting up domed cities of sterile glass and plastic which reared in startling contrast to the gaping pits of tremendous workings.

Durgan watched as they landed, seeing men tending machines, ant-like in their ordered confusion, slave-like in their dependence on one or the other of the great combines which owned the satellite and permitted grudging entry to those unattached. Yet despite their control some freedom remained. The freedom to range outside the cities and workings, to starve for want of employment, to die unnoticed and ignored.

In a small room in one of the featureless buildings Durgan met the man who held all the answers.

He was a small, wrinkled, shrewd-eyed man with a suit of expensive fiber and a heavy ring, which winked with flashing colors as he moved his hand. He nodded to the girl, as she left, gestured towards a table loaded with a dozen kinds of liquor.

"You are a drinking man, Mr. Durgan. What is your pleasure?"

"Brandy," said Durgan and added, "The real stuff. From Earth."

"A test, Mr. Durgan?" The man smiled. "If it is I can pass it. My name, by the way, is Creech. I take it that you are interested in my proposition?"

"I can tell you that when I've heard what it is." Durgan tasted his brandy, finding it insipid after *zulack*. "But, of course, you know how much I was told. Your messenger was most discreet."

"Not without reason." Creech took a chair, waited until his guest was seated and then said, "How are your nerves, Durgan?"

"Good enough."

"Good enough for what? Could you ride a bucket boat again?"

Could he dip once more into hell? Durgan leaned back, eyes veiled, listening again to the screaming threnody of Jupiter's atmosphere tearing at the skin of his boat, seeing the swirl and twist of vapor against the screens, feeling the bucking confusion and horrible disorientation. Each ride had been a gamble. Every trip had meant running the gauntlet with death waiting a hairsbreadth away. To ride a stream of fire down into the tremendous gaseous envelope, to level out at a selected depth, to trip the opening of the bucket, the huge plastic envelope trailing after the vessel, to cram it full of compressed gases, ammonia, methane, hydrogen even, a slew of elements waiting to be gathered, to seal the bucket and then to drag it up and out of the atmosphere and back to the depot on Amalthea.

Could he do it again?

"They said I was past it. That my reflexes had grown too slow. They ended my contract on three days' notice."

Creech leaned forward. "Did you agree with them?"

"No."

"But there was more, wasn't there? The last trip you took. You returned empty. Why?"

"I hit a bad spot. The convection currents were all to hell. When I tried to level out I couldn't hold the boat steady enough to open the bucket. Had I tried it would have dragged me out of control. So I gave up and got out."

"Right out." Creech bit thoughtfully at his lower lip. "I've read the psych-reports and they say you lost your nerve. That you turned coward. That you aborted the dip without really giving yourself a chance. Are they wrong?"

Durgan looked at his brandy then set aside the glass.

"They weren't down there," he said. "They didn't feel what I felt. All they had to go on was the relayed instrument-readings and they aren't to be trusted. I could have taken a gamble and probably died because of it. I figured that it was better to be a live coward than a dead hero. Alive I could try again. Dead they would have lost the boat."

"And so they kicked you out. You went to Ganymede and lived as a harvester." Creech picked up the glass of brandy and handed it back to Durgan. "Drink it. It may be your last for some time."

"Meaning?"

"I've got a job for you. I'll say it quick. I want you to drop down to the bottom. To hit the core of Jupiter. Right down through the envelope until you reach solid ground."

"No," said Durgan.

"You mean you won't do it?"

"I mean that it can't be done. Can you even begin to realize what the pressure is like down there? The bottoms of terrestrial oceans would be a vacuum in comparison. Down there hydrogen and nitrogen would be compressed into liquid ammonia, the—"

"I know about the pressure," interrupted Creech. "And about the gravity, two and a half Earth normal, but it can be done and I have the vessel to do it. All I need is a pilot with guts enough to handle it. Guts and experience so that he can ride the winds and stay in one piece. In return I'll make that man rich for life."

Durgan looked at his glass, at the brandy it contained. A bottle of the stuff would cost more than he could harvest in a week. The girl hadn't lied, she had shown him the jackpot, from now on it was up to him if he hoped to collect.

Quietly he said, "When do I learn the rest?"

"You don't. Not unless you agree to ride all the way. Bucket riders are scarce, most of them die young and the rest are broken. You didn't break.

The fact that you managed to survive on Ganymede proves that. That's why I sent for you. Are you with me?"

"You've got yourself a pilot," said Durgan. And swallowed the brandy.

It was an old and familiar dream. A hand was pressing him down hard against the ground and it kept on pressing. His chest collapsed, the broken ends of shattered ribs lacerating his lungs, his intestines squashed into a messy pulp, the bones of his skull began to yield but still the giant hand kept pressing, pressing, grinding against skin and bone until he was nothing but a red smear on the dirt.

And still the hand kept pressing until there was nothing but a liquid trace, cells imploding, molecules crumpling, elements forced together to make new compounds.

And the worst part was that he was still alive, still aware and able to feel.

It wouldn't be like that, Durgan knew. If the hull was breached death would be instantaneous, a blast of pressure which would paste him against the metal before he would have time to even guess at what was happening. But the cold knowledge brought little comfort. Imagination still continued to haunt him with speculations of what might happen, what would happen if something went wrong.

The others didn't appear to be worried.

Nanset was the engineer, a quiet, scholarly-looking man who wore contact lenses and spoke in a voice barely more than a whisper. Pendris was different, a tough veteran of the Jovian moons, a hard man with calculating eyes and the muscles of a bull. His job was to operate the waldos.

Creech made the introductions then retreated to stand beside a screen. Sheila took a position beside a projector, a warm touch of color in the otherwise spartan furnishings of the room.

"Now that we have all met I want to brief you on what has to be done." Creech's dry, emotionless voice was swallowed by the soundproofing of the chamber. "As you know we are going to send a vessel down to the solid core of Jupiter. Nanset has assured me that his force-field will provide ample protection against the pressure and, as his own neck will be involved, I tend to believe him. Aside from that the vessel has been reinforced with multiple hulls to allow for a cascade accumulation against external pressure. To adjust the build-up will be Pendris's job. Durgan, naturally, will be the pilot. The nature of the operation is basically simple.

We are going to salvage a lost cargo."

He snapped his fingers as light and color glowed from the screen, flight paths traced in strands of white, red dots moving to illustrate his explanation.

"A few months ago a ship of the United Combines set out for Earth. Unfortunately, it was hit by a scrap of uncharted debris that contained sufficient velocity to throw the vessel towards Jupiter. The heat-energy generated by the impact fused the drive-system and, helpless, the ship fell into the atmosphere. Before being destroyed the crew managed to arrange a continuous-message broadcast and the descent of the stricken vessel was monitored all the way down to just before the final landing. The cargo was, and is, extremely valuable. Recovery will ensure that we all gain rich rewards."

Put like that it was simple, idiotically so. Durgan glanced from one to the other of his crew and when neither mentioned the obvious did so himself.

"Jupiter isn't a small place. You're talking of something which has close to twenty-five thousand million square miles of solid surface area."

Creech turned from the screen. "I know that."

"Radio transmissions from the planet aren't reliable. If you're hoping that cross-bearings determined the crash-point then you're hoping for too much."

"I realize that also." Creech was unflustered. "Fortunately we don't have to depend on dead-reckoning, radio fixes or educated guesses. The entire descent of the vessel was computerized and the probable crash-point determined to within five square miles." He snapped his fingers before Durgan could say more. The picture on the screen changed to that of a space ship.

"The *Archimedes*," said Creech. "The vessel that crashed. You will note that it is a normal interplanetary transport with capabilities for carrying both cargo and passengers. No passengers were carried on its last journey. A special cargo container was fitted within the hull and occupied this space." His hand tapped the screen. "I think it safe to presume that the vanes carrying the guiding jets would have been ripped from the structure within a short while after entering the atmosphere. I think we can also assume that the crash with the meteor weakened the rear so that too would have been torn free. The remainder, together with the cargo container, most probably fell as a single unit, perhaps disintegrating on landing."

He paused as if expecting objections and, when he received none, continued.

"It may be necessary to cut free the cargo container and the salvage vessel has been provided with means to do so. You will also be provided with power-assisted suits to enable you to move in the high gravity. Continuous scrambled-beam radio transmission will be maintained during the entire flight. Miss Moray will take care of communications. Have any of you any questions?'

Pendris lifted his voice. "Do we get a chance of some training? If I'm to handle unfamiliar devices in a hostile environment I'd like to check them out before we start."

"This is only a preliminary briefing. You will have ample time to do as you suggest."

Durgan said, "I'm not happy about the crash-point area. It's too large. Five square miles is a lot of territory when you're relying on naked-eye vision—and in the soup you don't see far at the best of times. Is there any way of narrowing the field?"

"There is. I will tell you about it later."

"All right, I'll accept that, but what about the computerized landing? Down low conditions are unknown so how could a machine have determined the correct flight-path?"

"It did. You must take my word for it."

Nanset whispered, "This cargo. Supposing the container has burst and scattered the contents. How will we recognize it?"

"I'll tell you that just before you leave." Creech nodded to the girl and the screen went blank as she turned off the projector. "From now on you stay together. You talk to no one and you go nowhere without my permission. Is that perfectly clear?"

"In other words we're prisoners," said Durgan grimly.

"You object?"

"I object to a lot of things and one of them is putting my head on a block. But making a fortune is something I like. For that I'm prepared to play along but I like to know what the rewards are."

Creech met his eyes. "I promised you all that you will be rich for life."

"Rich is just a word and for me it isn't good enough. How about some figures?"

"Five million," said Sheila from where she stood behind the projector. "Five million for each of you. Good enough?"

Pendris whistled. "For me, yes."

Nanset blinked. Durgan turned to face the girl and met her cool stare.

"The jackpot," she said. "That's what I promised and that's what you'll get. Any more questions?"

"One," said Durgan. "Where is the ship?"

"On Europa." Creech stepped from the screen. "We'll be there in three days time."

Europa, half the mass of Luna, almost half a million miles from the heart of Jupiter, a place of eroded stone and crumbling rock. A small place with sheds and workshops, electric furnaces burning their way into the metallic heart, atomic engines spewing out heat and light and slugs of fuel for the engines that sent the ships across the void.

A rough place with the great disc of Jupiter filling the sky at night and the sun a pin-point at day. Airless, barren, a disposal dump for unwanted scrap. An ideal place in which to convert a ship in privacy.

Durgan checked it inch by inch.

It was an adapted bucket boat, the massive hull reinforced by four extra sets of plating each removed from the other by thick stanchions. The engines had been removed, the cabin space reduced, the bucket controls and housing sealed. In the increased space new engines had been fitted giving three times the original power. Sheathed in external housings the waldo attachments broke the smooth contours. The stubby wings to grip and ride the atmosphere were like the feathers on an arrow.

As he worked Durgan brooded. The ship had cost money, the conversions more. Whatever the cargo was that Creech hoped to salvage must be of immense value. Something to justify the essential investment of equipment. He spoke about it to the girl.

"It's none of your business," said Sheila. "Believe that, Brad. Just do the job you've contracted to do and forget the rest."

"I can't."

"Why not? Are you so rich you can afford to throw away five million?"

"What five million?" They were sitting beneath a dome of transparent plastic, drinking coffee imported from the Inner Worlds, listening to music recorded a century before. The glow of Jupiter-light cast colored shadows on the pale contours of her face, touched her hair with transient gleams. "You can't lose what you've never had so what the hell are you talking about?"

"Forget it, Brad. Take what life brings and stop arguing. Look on it as just another job."

"Is that what you think it is?" He looked up at the glowing face of the planet. Tonight the Red Spot was unusually bright. "Look at it. All you can see is the upper limits of the atmosphere but try to imagine what it's like lower down. Or, if you can't do that, go and see some of the bucket boat riders. You'll find them in the psycho wards scared of a shadow, unable to stand even the pressure of a sheet. That's the way it gets you in the end."

"So what?"

"So I want to know what all this is about. Where Creech comes in. What part you have in it all. And don't tell me that you're just a messenger. That worked once but it won't work again. Give, girl, or look for another pilot!"

"He'll kill you," she said emotionlessly. "If you back out now Creech will have you gunned down."

"Maybe." Durgan was grim. "He can try but if he doesn't make it the first time he'll never get a second chance—and you'll still need a pilot." The music changed, the thrumming beat of rock smoothing into the strumming melody of cadenza, achingly poignant with the thin wail of pipes, the repetitious beat of drums. On the far side of the dome a woman began to shiver in sympathetic response.

Sheila drank the last of her coffee. "Would you really back out, Brad?"

"Quit playing!" He was getting angry, his own nervous responses reacting to the emotional throb of the music. "I'm not a kid to be fed on promises of candy. What is this deal, anyway? Straight salvage or a straight steal?"

He caught the expression in her eyes, the minute tightening of muscles, the cautious veil. Abruptly he was calm, his anger dissipating at the result of his probe.

"I guessed," he said, "but I want you to say it. No one offers the kind of money you mentioned for a legitimate operation. Now talk!"

"Give me a minute." She looked at her empty cup. "I could use some more coffee."

And time to think up a story, he thought, but made no comment. From the automat he drew two cups, pausing on the way back as the woman across the dome began to scream. She sat, quivering, eyes glazed and a thin trickle of saliva running from her mouth. Her cries were sharp discordant, unthinking. The insidious beat of the cadenza had gripped her, jarring her nervous system, warring with the regular beat of her heart.

Durgan crossed to her table, set down the cups of coffee and slapped her sharply across the cheek.

"What—" The screaming died as she sat, blinking, one hand rising to the place he had struck. "What's the matter?"

"It got you," he explained. "The music. Either move or break the circle. Think of something pleasant, talk to someone, look outside."

Her eyes measured his height, the planes of his face, registered an unmistakable invitation.

"Talk, you said. With you?"

"Not me." He picked up the cups. "I'm busy."

Sheila looked at him as he sat down, her eyes moving from his face to the woman. "A hell of a way to snap her out of it. Aren't you ever gentle?"

"When I've got the time, yes. Now I haven't got the time. You were going to tell me something. Let's get on with it."

She toyed with her cup, very beautiful, very alluring, her femininity enhanced by the colored shadows, the primitive impact of the music. Twice he caught the movement of her eyes, the subtle hesitation, then she made her decision.

"I'll give you the truth, Brad, and it is the truth no matter what else you might hear. The ship was carrying a cargo from the United Combines. It was a year's production of *shedeena* crystals. I shouldn't have to tell you what they are. Callisto is unique in its core-formation. The crystals, some say, are the result of divergent pressures existing way back when the solar system was first created. Others tend to think that Callisto might be a stellar wanderer caught in Jupiter's gravity well—but none of that really matters. Callisto is the only source of the crystals. The various companies holding franchises are forced to work together and pool their harvest. In all other matters they work as separate units but not in this. You can guess why."

"A price ring," said Durgan thickly. "More. The only way in which they can avoid mutual warfare. A year's production, you say?"

"Yes."

He looked down at his hand. It was trembling a little, the coffee in the cup he was holding shimmering as it caught the light from above. A year's supply! Why they had allowed it to accumulate didn't matter. To force up the price, to ensure security, to gather a full working load—none of it mattered. All that was important was that the *shedeena* crystals were an anti-agathic, an anti-death drug which enabled the old, the rich, the influential to gain renewed youth and extended virility. Immortality, perhaps, if the supply could be maintained.

A year's supply!

Its value was incalculable. How much is life worth to a rich and dying man? What concessions would a ruler grant to the one who could deliver the source of longevity?

"Sometimes it happens," said Sheila quietly. "A combination of events that opens the door to everything you've ever dreamed about. I saw my chance and took it. When the ship was hit everyone seemed to go crazy. I was monitoring the flight and operating the computer. I kept track of the fall until the information ceased coming in—and then I made a couple of alterations. The information the combines have is useless. Only I have the true position of the wreck."

"And Creech?"

"The money-man, the fixer, the one who figured out what to do. He's clever, Brad. He waited just long enough to make sure that I was telling the truth and then he acted. Then—"

Durgan was sharp. "How?"

"How what?"

"How did he know that you were telling the truth?" He answered his own question. "When they didn't find the cargo, naturally. There must have been attempts at salvage. The combines wouldn't leave that stuff lying about without trying to get it. How many attempts, girl?"

"Five."

"And?"

"Five failures. Three ships just disappeared. One aborted the mission when the crew lost their nerve. The other imploded two-thirds of the way down." She hesitated, then added, "All were using Nanset's force field."

"Which means it doesn't work," said Durgan. "Good news."

"It does work. At least he says it does and he's willing to risk his neck on it. According to him the other engineers didn't know how to adjust the compensating factor. He could be right. Everything was done in such a hurry that something could have been unchecked. And the pilots weren't as experienced as they might have been."

Hurry, he thought, and fear and the desire for secrecy. Bucket boat riders might have done the job but they were all under contract aside from those no longer fit. And no bucket rider in his right mind would have agreed to take a ship down so far.

22

Nanset said, "This really isn't necessary, Durgan. I can assure you that the field will give us ample protection."

"I like protection," said Durgan. "As much of it as I can get. That's why we're going to wear the suits from the beginning." His voice echoed in his ears and he remembered there was no need to project his words. The radio would do that.

"Engineers," said Pendris sourly. "Give me a field man every time."

"How the hell do you think we're going to move down there without the suits? Or did you figure we could get them on just before we land?"

"All right, I'll accept that, but why the increased pressure in the cabin? Surely we could wear the suits and leave the face-plates open?"

Durgan checked his instruments before replying. The ship handled well despite the alterations but, in space, that told little. The test would come when they hit the atmosphere and began to fight the winds.

"Protection," he said flatly. "Our internal pressure is as high as the fabric will take. We'll equalize it a few miles down but it will give us an advantage. Now shut up and let me get on with the job."

It had been the same in the old days. The voice of the monitor had been a source of irritation, a scratching at his concentration best ignored if he was to put all he had into the dangerous business ahead. Then he had ridden alone without others to keep informed. Now he was not alone but all else was the same. The darkness of star-shot space, the transmitted thrum of the tubes, the mounting tension as the great ball of Jupiter swam closer and closer until it filled both mind and vision.

"Monitor to ship. You are three degrees off course."

Sheila riding with Creech in an attendant vessel, checking his flight with her stolen data, hoping to guide him through a screaming hell of frozen gases and hit a minute bull's-eye far below.

Durgan acknowledged and returned to his concentration. At first it wouldn't be too bad, a slowing, a tendency to veer and twist, a mounting whine from beyond the hull. Then he would match speeds and begin to fall. The whine would increase, the juddering fight as winds tore at the vessel and negated the controls. To fight them was useless. The trick was to use them, to ride the streaming currents, using vanes and jets to maintain some measure of control. If he lost it the ship would spin, flung by mighty forces and turning end over end to be torn apart in shattered ruin.

He heard the sharp intake of breath as the winds caught them, sensed the tension of Nanset and Pendris as they gripped their couches. Strapped down they were relatively safe but he could understand their fear. The screens pictured a seething fog of fuming nightmare, the external friction a nerve-tearing whine.

It lessened a little as he matched velocities, ignoring the voice from his radio, knowing that he was off-course but knowing that he could do nothing about it for the moment. Durgan checked his instruments, the big red hand of the external pressure gauge centered in the panel, handling the ship automatically with the skill of hard-won experience.

"Prepare for first pressure-adjustment," he said to Pendris.

"System ready."

"Seal first compartment at double interior pressure."

Cascade accumulation, an elementary precaution if the weight could be spared, the weight and the extra power necessary provided. As they descended, the compartments between the hulls would be filled and sealed with gases of increasing pressure, each helping to bolster the metal skins against that outside. With four extra hulls and a highly pressurized cabin they would be able to withstand six times the pressure of a single hull.

Six times, a wide margin, but enough?

Durgan grunted as he rode the winds. Already he was down further than he had ever been before and now the ship seemed sluggish, the exterior density robbing it of easy manoeuvrability. And the old fear was growing. The knowledge that pressure mounted the lower he went until it would reach a million atmospheres.

"You are widely off-course." Sheila's voice reflected her strain. "Correct seven degrees north."

Durgan made the adjustment.

"Final compartment sealed." Pendris dropped his hands from the bank of controls before which he lay. "Now it's up to Nanset." He grunted as something rose beneath them and sent the ship into wild gyrations. "Durgan!"

He made no answer, hands dancing on the controls, jets of fire streaming from the tubes as he judged time and pressure. It was a thing impossible to teach and learned only by doing. The instinctive reaction of a trained pilot, a man who was almost a flesh and blood extension of his vessel.

As the ship settled he snapped to Nanset. "Activate your shield."

A faint blue shimmer spread throughout the cabin and vanished as it raced for the outer hull. A generator moaned as it took the strain, the note rising as the engineer made an adjustment.

"Field adjusted and operating at optimum level." Nanset's voice was confident. "Now we've nothing to worry about. The field is established on the fringe molecules and will take all this planet can give it. It's a form of stasis," he explained. "An energy-concept linked to the center of the generator. The higher the pressure the more power will automatically be fed into the field and, in a sense, the pressure is fighting itself. The function can best be expressed by the mathematical formula—"

"Forget it," said Pendris impatiently. "This is no time for a lecture. Just so long as it works I'll be satisfied. How much longer, Durgan, before we find the jackpot?"

"As long as it takes."

"Is that the best you can do?"

"Quit bothering me."

Pendris inhaled with a spiteful hiss. Thickly he said, "I'm in this too or have you forgotten?"

Durgan made no answer.

"Listen, you—"

"Shut your mouth!" Durgan snarled as he felt the ship twist and begin to spin. The last thing he wanted now was the idle chatter of fools! Sweat beaded his forehead and ran down his face as he struggled to maintain control. It stung his eyes, the raw patch on the side of his neck where the suit had chafed. Like a wild animal the vessel fought his control. Something struck against the hull with a dull reverberation. Fog plumed in the screens, parting to show frothing masses of vapor, uniting in coiling tendrils.

Nanset made a choking sound. "God!"

Something rose before them, tall, white, jagged with broken peaks. The engines roared as Durgan fed extra power into the jets, the ship tilting as he lifted the nose. For a moment they seemed to hang stationary and then the massed ice threw itself towards them, dropping as they climbed, exploding into raging steam at the touch of their blast.

And, suddenly, the vapor lifted, seeming to jerk upwards in a lowering bank of cloud beneath which they flew with flaring jets and clear vision.

"We've done it!" said Pendris. "By God, we've done it!"

Below them lay the solid mass of Jupiter.

It was a place of nightmare, the ebon darkness ripped by the ruby light of widespread volcanic activity, the crimson glow fanning out in feathered plumes of flaming gas. The scene brightened as Durgan adjusted the screens, utilizing the lower wavelengths of light, electronic magic converting them into the visible spectrum. Now they could see raging pools of liquid ammonia whipped into a frenzy by the tidal waves stemming from the spouting craters. The pools, small on Jupiter but large enough for seas on Earth, stretched between mountain chains of solid ice, blue and green and somber umber, shining with red and orange light from the burning gases. The glare of their own blast illuminated the landscape and caused long trails of incandescent vapor to writhe like serpents, green and yellow and brilliant red, twisting and coiling in enigmatic patterns.

"The heat is breaking down the elements," said Nanset quietly. "Cracking compounds locked for millions of years in frigid stasis. That's oxygen burning, and hydrogen and methane. Who knows what elements and how they will act down here?'

"Heat?" Pendris snorted his disgust. "What about all those volcanoes? The heat of our blast is nothing to them."

"Heat is relative. On Earth those volcanoes would be nothing. They wouldn't even get started. That stuff isn't water, remember, but liquid ammonia. Those mountains are of ice. The atmosphere must be a mixture of hydrogen, ammonia, methane and carbon tetrahydride. Interesting."

"Check your field," said Durgan sharply. "You've no time to gawk at the scenery. Pendris, get busy on the detector."

Creech had given them the instrument. A box fitted with dials, which, he claimed, would register the presence of the cargo. If they could get close enough. If it would work in the conditions existing under the clouds. If the cargo was still as it had been.

Durgan spoke into the radio.

"Sheila. We've reached bottom. Check my position."

"You moved off course. You should have stayed on it."

"A mountain got in the way. We—""

"Brad!" Her voice was strained. "Are you all right?"

"So far, yes. Now quit being polite and get on with the job. Direct me please. Direct!"

He fell silent as her professional drone came over the speaker, a string of co-ordinates, corrections, alterations. The ship thrummed as it moved in a wide circle, slowing as it met the head-on force of the wind which moved at a constant velocity over the ground, bucking as it met it side on.

Pendris sucked in his breath.

"Anything?"

"I'm not sure, Durgan. The needles kicked a bit. Can you go back over?"

"I'm spiraling. Keep a sharp watch and yell if you see anything. Nanset!"

"Yes?"

"How is the field holding out?"

"Fine." The engineer had lacked conviction. He enlarged the comment at Durgan's insistence. "We dropped a fraction back there. It shouldn't have happened but it did. Maybe the atmosphere is corroding the outer hull and thus building up resistance. I've made the necessary adjustments."

"The hull is corrosion-proof," said Pendris. "Stop making excuses and keep your attention on your machine. Right, Durgan?"

"That's good advice—why don't you follow it?"

"I'm doing just that." His voice was ugly. "But when we get out of here you and me are going to have a little talk in a dark alley. I don't go for snotty pilots."

Sheila spoke before Durgan could answer. "Have you located it yet, Brad?"

"No."

"What's keeping you?"

"Are you joking? It's a mess down here. We could be lucky and hit it right away or we could search for a hundred years. Is Creech riding you?"

"Well, he—"

"Tell him to get lost. Have you any more data I can use? No? Then quit babbling and let me get on with the job."

It was hard to talk with more than two gravities tearing at the muscles, making every movement an exercise in applied strength, and he was beginning to feel the strain. The suits helped but that help had to be paid for in sore places, a body slimed with perspiration, itches which couldn't be scratched, aches which couldn't be relieved. And it was impossible to forget the pressure outside, the giant hand which would crush him into a smear should something go wrong.

Durgan adjusted the controls, tightening the spiral pattern he had chosen, thinking of a falling ship and the variable forces that would play on it. A last-second shift of wind and it would have been carried miles from the anticipated crash-point. An abrupt loss of mass the same. Yet the girl had been adamant as to its location. He examined the screens, trying to catch a glimpse of twisted metal, the lines of something artificial and alien to the landscape below. He saw nothing but the fury of volcanic activity, the shimmer of disturbed seas, the red glow painted on curtains of glistening ice.

"There!" Pendris's voice was high with excitement. "We've just passed it. The needles damn near left the dials!"

The vessel shuddered as Durgan cut acceleration and turned to face back from where they had come.

"There!" said Pendris again. "There!"

A torrent of lava fell from the crest of a high ridge, falling into a pool sparkling with flecks of dying brilliance. To one side, almost hidden by a crusted mass of deposited crystals, a sheared plate of twisted metal shone in the ruby light.

The wreck of the *Archimedes*.

They found the cargo container a mile away lying in a patch of luminous snow, a thin green haze blurring fine detail. Incredibly it was still almost intact, the thick metal buckled and warped, torn in several places, the openings having prevented crushing implosion. Deftly Durgan steered the ship towards it, his hands delicate on the controls as he fed power to the jets, the outer hull slithering over the frozen surface.

"How's that, Pendris? Close enough?"

Pendris grunted. He sat upright, his helmet enclosed by an enfolding mask, both hands thrust deep into the gloves of the waldo attachments.

"Can you get it a bit closer?"

Power thrummed as the ship edged forward. Nanset looked up from his dials.

"We shouldn't make actual contact," he said. "The field is becoming unbalanced, the energies grounding from the area of contact."

"Can you compensate?"

"I'm trying. For a time, yes, I think I can manage it. But be quick."

Pendris grunted again. "Quick? The damned thing's covered with scrap. I'll have to cut it free before we can hope to fasten the grapnels."

"Then get on with it!" Durgan was sharp, worried, on edge now that he had nothing to do. Now they had arrived Pendris was the main factor.

"Don't waste time flapping your mouth!"

"I'll get you!" said Pendris. "When we get out of here I swear that I'll get you!"

"Anytime you fancy!" Durgan drew a shuddering breath. "Now get busy earning your pay!"

In the screen he could see the waldo attachments unfold from their housings, literal extensions of Pendris's hands and arms, stretching, reaching, bright fire blazing as lasers cut through jagged pieces of metal. From the operator's mask Pendris's voice came as a musing drone.

"Tough. The damned thing is built like a safe. Solid metal strapped and reinforced like the vault of a bank. Lucky for us in a way, that's why it stayed in one piece, but what the hell would they be carrying to take such precautions?"

The lasers died, were replaced by mechanical claws that ripped the tattered remains from the bulk of the container. A hook caught in one of the openings, pulled, dropped free as it made no impression. Again Pendris tried to turn the container, to shift it from its bed. A third failure and he swore in savage irritation.

"It's too heavy! Those walls must be six inches thick! Why the hell didn't Creech warn us?"

"Maybe he didn't know." Durgan leaned closer to the screen. As the container was situated it was impossible to weld grapnels and hope to lift it from the planet. The strain would be too great. "Maybe I can use the ship to turn it. Lift your waldos and I'll try."

Nanset warned, "I'm getting close to maximum output."

"Keep a five per cent safety margin," said Durgan "When you reach it let me know." As the waldos lifted from the container he fed power to the jets, inching forward, using the bulk of the vessel to ram against the container. For a moment it resisted then suddenly gave. Durgan edged back and turned from the controls. "All right, Pendris Try again."

Once more the mechanical attachments clawed at the misshapen bulk. Pendris's drone was a mutter of rising frustration.

"It's no good. The thing is too damaged and too heavy. Maybe if I cut away the metal it might be possible to weld some grapnels to the interior."

Durgan said, "Can't you fix holding straps around the outside?"

"No. I can't manipulate it. If we try hooking direct to the box its own weight will tear it free before we've lifted a dozen miles. The entire thing is busted all to hell."

The hooks lifted and were replaced by the lasers. Sparks flew and molten droplets ran from yielding metal as the torches cut into the thick walls of the container. Pendris was an expert at his job. The searing beams answered to his expert manipulation, cutting just deep enough, flaring at carefully determined angles, dying before they could burn the interior. Again the hooks swung down, gripped lifted and tore the top of the box completely free.

From the interior of the container rose a cloud of vivid green vapor.

It spread, pluming, fanning as it rose, clinging to the waldo attachments, condensing into a nimbus of darkening emerald.

Pendris swore in sudden anger.

"What the hell? The damn waldos don't respond!"

The gas lifted again, thinning, coiling as it hovered over the opened container. It hung for a moment like a cloud and then moved again to settle beside the vessel.

"A chemical reaction," said Nanset. "It has to be. The heat of the lasers triggered off a progressive interaction probably converting crystals into gases and ending with a stable compound."

"Nice," sneered Pendris. His hands worked for a moment within the gloves then he turned from the mask, his face sweating behind the face-plate of his helmet. 'And what of the attachments?"

"They are activated by a series of interacting magnetic fields. It is possible that the gas has somehow neutralized the components." The engineer spoke as if he were addressing a classroom of students. "The thing is theoretically possible. An energized gas can be artificially generated down here, with the extreme pressure and alien chemistry it could happen naturally."

Durgan didn't join the discussion. He looked at the screens, at the exposed interior of the cargo container. The thing had been built to withstand any conceivable emergency. The exterior walls were merely the outer casing. Within, suspended on a mesh of springs and insulating baffles, hung a smaller box. Distorted, torn, but still in one piece. Inside would rest the *shedeena* crystals.

The largest fortune a man could hope to gain. Within sight. Within reach, almost, but with the waldos inoperative there was only one way it could be secured. This force field," said Durgan thickly. "Can it be applied to a suit?"

It was a gambler's throw with a fortune as the prize and a life as the stake and only a trickle of current providing the chance of success. If it should falter, the potential fall, a wire break, then death would be instantaneous.

Durgan tried not to think about it. He moved his left leg, the power-units of the suit accentuating his motion, enhancing his muscular power so that the limb moved, the foot lifted, fell with abrupt savageness beneath the clawing drag of a gravity which more than doubled his weight.

Beneath his boots the surface was rough, scored by the winds which tore past in a droning whine, pushing with savage intent.

Stooped over the cargo container Pendris lifted a wrapped slug of the precious crystals, using both hands, turning so as to allow Durgan to grip it with his left hand, pass it to where Nanset stood before the ship's open doors.

Light streamed from the interior, a warm, comforting glow, throwing distorted shadows over the eerie configurations of the Jovian landscape. More shadows moved as, far to one side, a gust of ruby flame stabbed through the darkness. Closer, from where the ruby stream fell from the crest to the pool of bubbling crimson, a dull glow shone, reflecting from the hull of the vessel, painting it with the uneasy color of blood.

Pendris's voice was harsh in the confines of the helmet.

"Awkward," he muttered. "I've got to stoop right over. Some of the wrappings are torn and there's more of that damned green gas."

A ball of it rose with him as he painfully straightened, clinging to the end of a slug, rising to wreath his suited arms. Mechanically Durgan took it, turned, passed it to Nanset. In a glowing pool at the side of the ship the green vapor that had streamed from the opened container rested like a smoky cloud of emerald. It seemed unaffected by the wind, streamers reaching to both ship and ground as if it clung with deliberate intent.

"Hurry," said Nanset. "I can't trust the generator to compensate on automatic for too long. Hurry!"

His voice shook a little and Durgan could understand his fear. He felt it himself. The unimaginable tons of pressure all around, the crushing force held back only by the magic of the force field. It revealed itself as a blue shimmer around the suits so that each man moved in a halo of nebulous light.

"Here!" Pendris held out yet another slug. "The damned stuff's getting harder to reach. It's padded all to hell." His breath sucked between his lips. "Money," he breathed. "A mansion on the Himalayas. Another at Polar North. Fine foods, women, the best of wine. My own ship, maybe!"

The lure that made them agree to take the insane gamble. Durgan had told them what the container held, dangling the bait of incredible wealth before their eyes, forcing the engineer to adapt his field to guard the suits. What did Nanset want, he wondered. A school of his own? A complete laboratory with money enough to staff it with the best brains available? A converted ship to plumb the secrets of Uranus?

Mechanically he passed on the slug.

The wind gusted, suddenly slamming with increased force against the ship, the men, the open container of the precious crystals. The ground shook a little, a low rumbling echoing through the helmets as the suits carried the grinding vibrations. Orange flame lifted to one side interspersed with shafts of vivid blue and the droning wind carried specks of dancing green. They swirled like snowflakes, like scraps of wispy cloud, meeting, uniting, growing into streamers of coiling vapor which clung to the suited figures, fogging the face-plates with emerald dazzle, passing to hang like gossamer from the ship and container.

Nanset's voice was a ragged whisper. "I don't like this. There's something strange down here, something terrifying. I get the impression that something is watching us."

"Shut up!" snapped Durgan. "There's nothing down here but gas and pressure."

"There could be life," insisted the engineer. "How do we know there isn't? The temperature is high enough for an ammonia-based metabolism. I—"

"Shut up and keep working!" Pendris snarled his impatience, fear edging his words. "Time for thinking is when we get out of here. Now move! Damn you, move!"

A blue ghost he lifted another slug, passed it to Durgan, who took it and handed it to the engineer. Nanset was clumsy. He stumbled and the slug fell from his hands into the pool of green vapor that clung stubbornly to the side of the vessel. He stopped to recover it, his hands plunging into the enigmatic mist. And vanished.

He disappeared like the flame of a blown-out candle. One second he was a blue-lined figure stooping, his arms wreathed with green. And then, instantly, there was nothing.

Nothing but a metallic smear edge with red, a paste of flesh and blood and bone, an ooze of organic and inorganic compounds from which trailed the wire which had fed his force field.

"God!" Pendris's voice echoed his terror. "What happened?"

"His field collapsed." Durgan fought his rising terror as he stood, afraid to move, afraid even to breathe for fear that any movement, no matter how slight, would send him after the engineer.

"His field— We've got to get out of here!"

Pendris turned from where he stood and began to move towards the open port of the vessel. Over the radio his breathing was harsh, ragged, the sound of a man on the edge of panic. Durgan caught his arm as he drew level.

"Wait!"

"Let me go! For God's sake, man! Let's get out of here!"

"Watch your feet! Break the wire and you'll die. Move carefully. If you fall who knows what might happen?" Durgan swallowed, hating the dryness of his mouth, the fear that sent sweat oozing from every pore. "Be careful, damn you! For God's sake go easy!"

Carefully he edged towards the open port, moving in inches, dying a hundred deaths at each tiny step. Always there had been the danger but now it had become horribly real. He had seen what the pressure could do, had actually seen it. Nanset had died before his very eyes!

He reached the edge of the port, climbed in, moved through the air lock and into the cabin. With exaggerated care he moved to the pilot's couch and called soft orders.

"Make sure that both wires are well within the cabin. Right?"

"Right."

"Then hit your couch. Fasten restraints. Right?"

Again Pendris said, "Right."

Durgan moved his hands. The outer door swung shut sealing the hull. The inner door followed to seal the cabin. The engines woke to life, the roar of power drumming with heavy vibrations through the vessel. On the screen the blast looked like a sword of impossibly brilliant flame.

Praying, his mouth filled with the taste of blood from his bitten lips, Durgan sent the ship streaking upwards from the Jovian terrain.

"Sheila to Brad. Come in Brad. Sheila to Brad. Come in Brad. Answer please. Answer, damn you! Sheila to Brad."

"Are you going to answer?" Pendris had caught the voice over the intersuit radio. His own was suggestive. "You don't have to. For all they know we died down there with Nanset."

"Watch your pressures!" Durgan concentrated on the instruments, the red hand of the gauge. He had relaxed a little now that they had risen well into the atmosphere, passing the danger point, the engines thrusting them even higher towards the empty cleanliness of space.

"Pressure compensated." Pendris operated his valves. "We won't explode. We can cut the field now and maybe get out of these damned suits."

"Not yet."

"Hell, why not? We're high enough for the hull to take normal pressure. "We've got solid oxygen in the tanks and all we need do is warm it and clear the cabin of accumulated gas. I'm sore," he complained. "And I itch like the devil. That ride up wasn't easy."

He hadn't known the half of it, his inexperience saving him from the worst. A man couldn't fear what he didn't know but Durgan had known all too well. He had ridden on his nerves, eyes strained as they checked the instruments, imagination cringing as he visualized what could so easily happen. A flaw, a single fragment of metal crystallizing beneath the pressure and vibration, anything and they would have joined the engineer in instantaneous extinction.

Now he rode the winds like an artificial bird, rising higher with each passing second, his relief an intoxication.

"Sheila to Brad. Come in Brad. For God's sake . . . , damn you! Sheila to Brad. Come in Brad."

"They're hungry," said Pendris. "Eager for the loot." His voice carried his disgust. "A lousy five million. That's all they wanted to pay for the price of a world. To hell with them!"

The ship bucked a little. Durgan steadied it and said, "You've got ideas?"

"Maybe." Pendris was cautious. "You going to clear the cabin? Give us some clear air to breathe?"

Durgan reached out and threw a couple of switches.

Heating coils would vaporise the stored blocks of solid oxygen. He would flush the cabin when the pressure grew high enough and when they had reached near-space. Then more blocks would provide a breathable atmosphere.

"Give it some time," he said. "These ideas of yours—what have you in mind?"

"You need me to spell it out? Hell, Durgan, you're no fool, you can recognize the big time when you see it." Pendris was eager. "That stuff we collected is worth how much? Sold legitimate a real bundle and sold under the counter a damn sight more. The combines alone would give us more than what Creech promised. And how do you know that he'll deliver? We've done the job and he won't need us any more. A couple of shots and he's saved a bundle. The girl too—she won't be needed either. We do the dirty work and Creech gets all the reward."

"We made a deal," said Durgan flatly.

"Sure we did—and it was completed when the waldos failed. From then on we were working for ourselves. Why else do you think we agreed to take that kind of a risk? You didn't spell it out, Durgan, but you didn't have to. The stuff's ours any way you want to look at it. We sweated for it and Nanset died getting it. I don't figure on letting it go."

"No," said Durgan. "I didn't think you would."

A lamp flashed on the panel. There was the thin whine of escaping air. On the screens the clouds suddenly thinned to wisps of vapor, fell as the ship continued to climb, merged with the misty ball of Jupiter. On a close orbit the ship swung over the mighty planet, building velocity so as to spiral from the savage tug of the gravity well.

"We'll be able to breathe soon," said Pendris. "Real air instead of this regenerated stink. What do you say, Durgan?"

"I'm thinking about it."

"What's there to think about? We've got our hands on the jackpot and all we need to do is to hang on to it. Creech? He can be taken care of. The girl? She's yours if you want her. I've a couple of contacts who can handle the sale and pay cash on the nail."

The lamp flashed again and a needle rose on a dial. Pendris grunted and lifted his hands to his face-plate. A gush of vapor came from within the suit as it opened, air heated by his own body-temperature, loaded with the moisture from his sweat.

Painfully he released the couch-restraints and swung his legs to the floor of the cabin. Moving awkwardly he began to divest himself of the cumbersome suit.

"I can't manage," he said. "Durgan, help me get out of this thing and I'll do the same for you."

Gloved hands jerked at the fastenings and they stepped from the harsh fabric and rigid construction of the suits.

Pendris looked a wreck. Blood seeped from raw patches on his hands and wrists, more from the side of his jaw. His face was red, lined with strain and fatigue, his eyes blood-shot, red-rimmed and angry. Durgan was in no better condition. He felt gritty and knew he stank. He needed a long, hot bath, a massage and about twenty hours sleep.

He turned to the controls as Pendris moved to the back of the cabin where the salvaged cargo was stored. The man was excited, eager to see what they had won.

"What do you think, Durgan? Should we rendezvous with Creech and take care of him? We could use his ship and he has the girl. Or maybe it would be better to let them both think we died trying." He laughed, a hoarse chuckle rasping from his sore lips. "Died! We damn near did at that. But it was worth it. Man! How it was worth it! When I think of all the things this stuff can buy—" His voice broke. "Durgan!"

"What is it?"

"Durgan! Look! What the hell—"

And then he screamed.

It was a harsh cry of an animal in both fear and pain. Durgan spun from the controls, the hairs prickling at the base of his neck, nerves tense for unexpected dangers.

"What the hell's the matter with you?"

Pendris didn't answer. He stood beside the pile of slugs reclaimed from the wrecked vessel, the compact bulk of *shedeena* crystals, staring with bulging eyes. Over the heaped pile, glowing in the cabin lights, a green vapor clung like a thin liquid, coiling, pulsing with a strange energy, rising in tenuous streams. More of the green vapor clung to his hands, puffy balls of brilliant emerald, clotted and writhing as it crawled up his arms.

"It burned," he whispered. "It stung like acid. I touched the slugs and it felt like fire. Durgan! Help me!"

"Step back! Away from the cargo! Stand back against the far bulkhead! Move, damn you! Move!"

Durgan reached back, his right hand diving beneath the instrument console, reappearing with the weight of a gun firmly clutched in his fingers.

"Insurance," he said. "I'm not such a fool as to trust others. I planted it when I examined the ship. If you or Creech had any bright ideas about cutting me out I intended to be ready." The muzzle of the weapon rose as Pendris made to step forward. "Stay where you are."

"You think I'm joking?" Pendris lifted his arms, balls of green fluffing like balls of emerald cotton, expanding as they climbed higher up his arms. "I tell you this stuff felt like acid."

"Try wiping the stuff off. Use one hand against the other." Durgan frowned as Pendris obeyed. "Jerk your arms. If it's a gas it should blow free."

It wasn't a gas or if it was it was like one he had never seen before. No matter how Pendris threshed his arms the vapor clung, clots of it catching his legs, his body. From the heap of slugs more gas rose to join that attached to the man. Within moments Pendris was covered in a green film that seemed to close around him, thickening, pulsing as with inner life.

"Durgan!" He stepped forward, stumbling, hands extended. "Durgan, help me!"

"Keep back!" Sweat beaded Durgan's face as he lifted his pistol. "Right back. Quick or I'll burn you apart!"

"You'd kill me?"

"If I have to, yes."

"You—""

"Save it," said Durgan sharply. "This is a tough life, Pendris, you've no cause to whine. How do you feel now?"

"I don't know. Just numb and weak." Pendris lifted his hands and pawed at his face. His voice was thin, cracked. "It's hard to breathe. For God's sake, do something!"

He lowered his hands and stood, swaying, thin tendrils of green vapor clinging tight to his body.

And, as Durgan watched, he aged.

He shriveled like a long-inflated balloon suddenly relieved of pressure. His face collapsed, prominent bone thrusting against skin that had grown sere and withered. His body stooped, his hands shrank to bony claws, a naked skull shone through thinning hair. His eyes glared from deep within shadowed sockets, lips parting to show-toothless gums. He stumbled forward, one step, then crumpled to the deck to lie like a heap of discarded clothing.

"Durgan!" His voice was a piping whisper. "Help me, Durgan! Help me!"

The hair vanished, the skin, the flesh beneath. Naked bone hung from the ends of the sleeves, the neck of the blouse. In the open sockets of the eyes green vapor rose in delicate plumes.

Durgan fired, jamming his finger hard against the trigger, sending blasts of incinerating flame lancing across the cabin to where the skeleton lay. It flared, smoldered, burst into flame and smoke.

Durgan lowered the weapon. Behind him the control panel flashed with signal lights as automatic fans whined into life, clearing the smoke.

Over the assembled stacks of reclaimed slugs the emerald vapor rose until it reached the roof, recoiled, then rose again, clinging, surging over the metal as if it were a leech.

From the radio came the insistent voice. "Brad, come in please. Sheila to Brad. Brad, please answer."

Durgan ignored it, watching the advance of the alien gas, remembering where he had seen it before.

On Jupiter, the strange cloud which had streamed from the opened cargo container and which had settled beside the ship, remaining despite the wind which would have blown any normal accumulation of gas away. Nanset had touched it, reaching into it with both arms as he tried to recover the dropped slug, and Nanset had died. Pendris had touched it—and now Pendris was dead.

Life, thought Durgan. Alien. Spawned in the chemical brew that was the atmosphere of Jupiter. Or perhaps the cargo itself had provided the stimulus, the concentrated life-force which the *shedeena* crystals provided. Or perhaps the strange thing had merely been attracted to the source of so much life-giving energy. It didn't matter.

It must have come aboard as they entered the cabin, unnoticed, drawn perhaps by the lure of the collected slugs. The release of pressure could have stimulated it, the flood of oxygen speeding its metabolism. It was a life-feeder and hungry. It would always be hungry. It would destroy every living thing it touched, sucking the life-force as if it were a sponge, compressing a lifetime of normal living into moments. It had to be destroyed.

He fired again, spraying the cabin with searing flame, blasting the gas, the pile of slugs, the roof and deck and bulkhead. Metal glowed with red heat and the air grew stifling. But, when the gun was empty, the gas remained.

Thicker, the cloud larger, the green more intense. It lapped against the walls and billowed towards the control panel, the couches, to the place where Durgan stood. More avid now that it had fed, eager for fresh life, new life-force, added fuel so that it could grow and expand to—

To cover a world if it were released on a planet. To hang waiting in space if he released it into the void. Hanging and drifting to, perhaps, be caught in a gravity well and be drawn down to Callisto or Ganymede, to maybe even reach Earth in time. A sea of emerald vapor to replace the blue seas, the white clouds, the rich brown of fertile soil.

"Brad!" Sheila's voice was ragged with strain. "For God's sake come in, Brad! Come in!"

Come in to warmth and safety, to luxury and the comforting softness of a woman's arms. And then he saw her, tall and lovely, her hair a golden curtain to her rounded shoulders, a green vapor touching, clinging, sucking away her youth, her beauty, her very life.

He looked down at his hand. On the back a spot of green swelled as he watched, spreading with a touch of fire, the pain instantly dying as the nerves were killed, the skin numbed and rendered senseless. A parasite, insidious, beautiful in a way but still a parasite. A freak of life, which with luck, would never be repeated.

The ship drummed as he sat before the controls and adjusted the power. In the screens the swollen ball of Jupiter rose as he dived towards it, the tenuous masses of upper-cloud ripped and torn by the savage winds. They closed around the vessel, whipping, streaming, the sound of their passing a droning thunder against the hull.

He would not hear them for long. Nor would he feel the sudden implosion which would send the ship and what it contained down to where it belonged.

The Red Spot made a wonderful target.

DREAMBOAT

Sydney J. Bounds

Dr. Walberg, ballpoint poised above a new notebook, sat just behind the couch. A young man lay relaxed on the couch, his eyes closed, smiling beatifically.

"All right, Danny," Walberg touched the young man lightly on the shoulder. "Tell me about your dream."

The silence lengthened in the room with pale gray walls before Danny began, his voice pitched low: "I'm in a boat, a small boat, a sailing dinghy, at sea. It's a big sea, gray and choppy, and I'm quite alone. I'm sailing well, riding the waves effortlessly. There's no horizon, the sea merges into the sky . . .

"The sail, a plain white sail, grows steadily larger. It's very big, towering over me, glistening like metal in the sunlight, and the water falls away beneath the keel. The boat's changing too—I'm in a sort of capsule." Danny's voice lifted, quickened. "Now I'm sailing through the sky, high up. The earth is a faded brown ball, like a coconut, and the sun huge and. flaming orange. The sky is deep violet, almost black . . .

"There are rocks in the sky. I'm passing a ringed world, and the rings glow like chips of blue-white ice in the darkness. Beyond, I can see a blaze of stars—not twinkling—but steady and bright and all the colors of the rainbow. It's peaceful here. The wind comes from the sun, driving me along, filling the sail and driving me out towards the stars . . .

"Looking up through the window in my capsule, I see the sail, truly enormous now and. gleaming silver with a gossamer-sheer rigging. I'm sailing across space in my boat, star-bound, sailing on and on, forever and ever, faster and faster. It's exhilarating, the most wonderful experience I've ever known."

A furrow of anxiety grooved Dr. Walberg's forehead. Danny was getting too excited, too deeply immersed in his fantasy. He interrupted: "Danny! This is merely a form of escape, you know that, don't you?"

"Yes doctor . . . I'm scudding along before the wind of space, heading out to the stars—"

Walberg said severely: "No, Danny, not *to* anywhere. You're running away, running from real life with its problems. Do you remember telling me, earlier, how you used to go sailing at weekends before you married? You're withdrawing from your responsibilities, trying to go back to bachelor freedom. It's time you faced reality."

"I'm looking at the stars, sparkling like gems scattered across the sea of space. *This* is real!"

"Your marriage is real, Danny. You married very young, to a woman older than yourself, and the glamor's worn off. A rep's job doesn't suit your temperament. You regret marrying and escape in your dream."

"You're so right, doctor! I *am* escaping, and I like it fine. There's no tension out here, no one nagging me. It's all smooth sailing—she handles well and I can do anything with her. Right now, I'm heading into a brightly-lit gas cloud, a shining hole in the sky. I've got stars to port and starboard, red and green. And speed, I'm really building speed all the time, fairly scudding along, going places for the first time in my life. I'm the captain, the responsibility's mine alone. Trimming sail now, tacking down a street of stars . . . there's a crosswind sprung up from somewhere, dark clouds blotting out guide lights. A storm! I'm being blown off course."

"Danny—"

"Don't worry, doc, I can handle her! We're coming round . . . sailing through a dark and gloomy place."

A shudder racked the young man on the couch. Walberg saw his eyes screw shut, his hands clench. "That's real life intruding, Danny. You're facing a crisis."

Danny began to sob. His words came thickly. "Stars fading . . . it's dark . . . dark . . . "

Walberg spoke softly. "This crisis of yours, Danny—your wife threatened to go see your boss. She wants to know why you haven't been promoted. She's going to demand you get a raise. You don't like the idea of her interfering, showing you up in the office. *This* is your problem, Danny. How are you going to deal with it?"

The man on the couch relaxed slowly. The beatific smile returned to his young face. "The stars! I can see them again, green, green like emeralds. The storm's over and I've ridden it out—that makes me a master mariner I guess. There's one star dead ahead, brighter than all the others, like an island in the sky and I'm making for it. It beckons me—"

Walberg said, urgently: "Danny! Danny, come back—you must face reality."

It seemed to the doctor that the room shimmered and a breeze blew across his face. He stared at the couch, where Danny's body appeared to lose solidity. He blinked rapidly.

"Danny . . . !"

The body on the couch continued to fade, became gray and misty. Danny's voice remained a few seconds longer, disembodied, floating down from a point above Walberg's head:

"This *is* reality, doctor, the good life, sailing into in to harbor at the end of a long voyage. I see the island clearly now, a blue sky and smooth water, breakers rolling gently onto golden sand. Trees. And a girl among the trees, waiting . . . I like it here. I'm going down, landing . . . landing . . . "

His voice faded and was gone.

In the silence of the room with pale gray walls, Dr. Walberg rose, stiff and trembling. Danny had solved his problem.

The couch was empty.

THE GUNMAN

Philip E. High

Needless to say, the formula in any state was illegal.

It had been discovered and stolen by a research chemist working for one of the big combines in the West.

He was well aware that the formula, given to his employers, would bring him little or no reward. Handled illegally and to the right people, however would bring rich rewards.

The formula, in liquid state, could be contained in a capsule no bigger than the normal pill.

Dropped into a glass of water, the capsule would dissolve in eight seconds.

It was colorless, odorless and tasteless.

Best of all, it was not a poison.

Any unfortunate deaths that might occur could never be traced to its use.

The actual results were obscure yet devastating.

No, not insanity, just change. The recipients remained, outwardly, as before and quite rational and exhibited no symptom that a psychiatrist could pin down.

For example, a well-known business magnate sold his business outright and joined a religious organization.

It is, perhaps, fortuitous, that this got several financially involved directors off the hook.

Adam Wenstone was chief director and absolute owner of a large business complex in the East.

His father had escaped the normal Inheritance Tax by passing the business on to his son at the age of seventy.

It was a sound business, and making a steady profit but there were those among the directors who thought it could do better. The number of opportunities which had cropped up and had somehow been missed!

So great had been the opportunities that two of the Directors had seen fit to take secret gambles of their own—with the firm's money.

Good God, who could have foreseen that Maxtrose investments would go down the pan overnight leaving nothing?

If only a greater part of the business was left to the other directors. With time and a little ducking and weaving they might have kept the inevitable at bay for long enough to recoup the loss but not with Wenstone in control. He checked and re-checked regularly and took painstaking computer surveys.

Desperate, Argyle and Martin, the two directors, snatched at the only straw which had become available to them.

"Are you absolutely sure this bloody stuff will work? Martin wiped his sweaty palms with a handkerchief.

"For the tenth time man, not absolutely sure. Nothing is absolutely sure, you must know that."

"Suppose it fails?"

"It has succeeded on twelve occasions so I see no reason for it to fail now. On the other hand, since you keep pushing it, I have taken alternative measures."

Martin dabbed at his palms again. "What other alternative—?" He stopped, his face pale. "You wouldn't dare."

"Can you think of anything better? After all, we only have to resort to it if this formula fails."

Adam Wenstone was thirty-three, slim and fit. Outwardly gentle and easy-going; he had an astute mind and was interested in many things but riotous living was not one of them.

Yet he awoke on that particular morning with the smell and the distinct taste of liquor in his mouth.

He tried to open his eyes and they refused to open.

He was conscious again of the smells and tried to identify them. Horses, yes, no mistake about that; there was one near somewhere.

He came back to the liquor again. How? He was teetotal. Yet somehow, in an odd way, his body felt as if it was used to it and liked it.

His senses returned to the smell, a disgusting mixture of horse, sweat and unwashed body.

It was his body and it stank.

His arm shifted but he hadn't shifted it.

He thought: "God, I feel like hell this morning."

They were his thoughts but he hadn't thought them.

He was suddenly very much afraid but he kept a grip on himself because it was clear that there was nothing he could do about it.

He was trapped somewhere and, at the moment there was nothing he could do to escape.

He tried to speak but could make no sound.

He tried to direct a thought message: *"Can you hear me?"* but there was no response.

His head itched. He could feel fingers scratch the itch and feel the fingers scratching but not by him.

He could feel every inch of his body, every twitch and breath but he had no control over it.

He thought: *"That Mex is real fast, I'll have trouble there."*

They were not his thoughts, they had not come from him, yet he understood what the thoughts implied. The dark skinned man from over the border had come in for a fight, a challenge.

Adam Wenstone was an intelligent man and already had an outline of his situation. Somehow—be it illusion or something else—he was occupying, and sharing, the body and mind of another man.

The other man was the host occupant while he, Adam, was the passenger.

The host was in absolute control. When he wanted to move, he moved. He, Adam, could feel and experience what was happening but that was all.

He knew every thought of the host, knew everything the host knew but, again, could do nothing about it.

On the other hand, the host had no idea that he had taken another intelligence on board, who was sharing his life with him.

The host opened his eyes and Adam saw that he was in a crude wooden shed. Two tethered horses shifted and stamped at the far end and he, the host, was lying on a sort of crude shelf on the opposite side.

Adam knew, because his host knew, that this was Jake's place.

The wide door swung open with a creaking sound and a man came in.

"I got you something to eat, bacon, beans and that. I'll try and get you some coffee later when Mom's place gets open.

"I'll pay you back."

"You always do, Limpy, but I'm worried about this Mex, he's Godawful fast. Buxton is offering four to one against you."

Adam, at the time, was only half listening. His host was fully awake and conscious and awake, his mind was open.

There was no need to see outside the shed, the whole picture was there, now part of Adam's knowledge and memories.

Mentally Adam's mind almost revolted. What was this, besides everything else—time travel?

This was a sleepy, one-horse town, settled in the curve of a wide river yet close to the railroad.

It had a wide dirt street lined by wooden shacks with only a few rising to two stories.

Adam had seen a large number of such streets in Westerns but there the picture had stopped. The film could not convey the smell of horses, wood smoke and most certainly not the flies. Dear God, the flies! On some days they swirled so thickly they blurred the vision. They covered the face, explored the corners of the eyes and probed the mouth and nostrils.

It caused his host no great irritation. It was part of life, like the fleas, the lice and, at night, of course, the skeeters. One slapped a few and squashed them flat but, always, a fair number got through and sucked their fill of blood.

Adam realized suddenly that he was being biased. If this was, somehow, time travel, then the great cities of the world were very little different.

The majority of the inhabitants were also lousy. Most of the bedrooms were filled with cockroaches and excreted the sour and sickly smell of bed bugs. Many of the streets held open sewers and rats ran openly across the road.

Beyond this town, however, was the open country with the soft river smells, grasses, wild flowers and the scent of pine.

Adam's host climbed to his feet and took a few uncertain steps. Limpy had broken his leg at the age of thirteen and had limped ever since. 'Doc' Munsen had fixed it as best he knew how but it was not one of his specialities. The broken bone had knit O.K. but somehow the leg had got shorter. Again the foot would not go flat to the ground properly.

Munsen, however, was still known as Doc because he had a half-breed woman who made concoctions out of herbs and suchlike. The stuff was very good for saddle sores, rope burns and things like that. Quite often—although his host had no knowledge of them—they stopped dangerous infections dead in their tracks.

His host ate then limped out into street. Cotter, the local storeowner, had kindly taken his horse when he had been too drunk to find it, let alone mount the damn thing.

A short way up the street, a tall man in a striped apron shouted a greeting, and added: "Goin' to take that Mex tonight, Limpy?"

"I reckon."

Adam was a little taken aback by his host's answer. It implied a subtlety which he had not suspected in the man. It was not a boast yet suggested confidence. It was, on the face of it, a wholly neutral observation that could be taken either way.

Adam had thought, at first, that his host was little more than an oaf with a horse and a gun, but nothing could be further from the truth.

Limpy had principles. He believed that women and children should be protected at any cost. His given word was an oath he would never break and he was unshakably loyal to his friends.

Then, of course, there were horses. After a minute or so, Adam became convinced that this man knew more about horses than the greatest race trainers and breeders of his own age.

He not only *knew* about horses, he felt, loved and understood them, He was often employed to break one in. Sometimes he got thrown a few times but he always won through by love and persistence, never by violence.

"If Limpy breaks one in, it's broke, you can take my word for it."

Somehow all this failed to fit in with the portrait of a gunslinger but Adam could see the complete picture.

Limpy had not gone out looking for a fight. He carried six-guns from habit and necessity as most them did but he had never fired them in anger.

Limpy had killed ten men and the first had been a traveling gambler with a green eye shade and a greasy pack of marked cards.

The gambler moved from township to township, staying only a night but cleaning up before moving on.

Limpy was only eighteen then and it was his first killing.

47

It was in the saloon and one of the painted girls from the house down the road was powdering her facer near the stable.

Perhaps she caught a reflection in her mirror or just saw something from the corner of her eyes but she said: "This bastard is switching cards!"

The gambler reacted, this was not the first time he had been caught out and had been forced to shoot his way out of a situation.

The set-up looked easy enough, not many in the saloon as yet. A group with their backs to him playing cards by themselves in the corner. Four elderly men at the bar and three girls, including the one near him, was all he had to contend with.

There was, of course, the fresh faced kid on the opposite side of the table. He'd already taken him for three dollars anyway.

The gambler swung back his jacket and reached for his guns. He'd kill the girl first, experience had taught him that killing a woman, no matter what she was, always caused diversion and delay.

The gambler had only just got his guns clear of their holsters when he got hit.

Limpy, holding cards in his left hand, had been scratching his upper thigh when the gambler reached.

The single shot punched the gambler and his chair over backwards and tumbled them to the floor.

Limpy looked down at the dead man and tried not to be sick. There was a hole in the man's chest, blood trickled from his open mouth and his eyes were still open. Somehow the eyeshade had come down his face and lay across his nose creating a grotesque effect.

Limpy felt no triumph, only a sort of gut-shock, he was shivering and shaking. It seemed to him that even his bad leg had begun to hurt a mite.

"He was going to kill me," said the girl. "I sort of sensed it inside me like."

She turned to Limpy. "I owe you, boy, really owe you. You can come and see me any time, *any time*. Won't cost you nothing."

Again, Adam was amazed. His host might have been forgiven for a feeling of triumph, but he felt only regret. It was kill or be killed, himself and the girl but he didn't like killing and never learned to like it.

Four weeks later a man burst into the saloon one Sunday evening but this was no gun duel, this was revenge.

"Where's the murdering bastard what killed my brother?" He carried a heavy shotgun, pointed. "I'm looking for a guy what limps. You lot at the bar there, stand clear of him or you'll get it too."

Only one reaction was possible. Limpy dropped flat and fired from the floor.

The man with shotgun dropped it before he could pull the trigger. He staggered, his face registering mild surprise, then he coughed blood and fell sideways.

Number three was a youth from a nearby township who fancied himself as a gun slinger. With a little more practice he'd go bounty killing.

He provoked and provoked. "What's the matter, you yeller livered bastard—draw!"

He made the mistake of reaching for his guns himself but was too slow to clear his holsters.

The memories and experiences of his host's life were now completely Adams', as if he had lived two lives. He was, however, still fumbling for an explanation. This life he was living now was *real* although he could take no active part in it. Was he telepathically or hypnotically attuned to the man? If so, why the past? He could make no sense of it.

He had ceased to be afraid aside from a few vague apprehensions. He had almost convinced himself that he was the victim of some curious circumstance that would right itself in time. In all probability he was the victim of some accident which had mentally induced the whole business.

He was almost happy in it and grateful that he had acquired such a vast range of additional knowledge almost without effort.

He could survive in the wilderness out there, if forced, without weapons. He could make fire, strike out for a certain destination without a compass, and read terrain by a mere glance.

Each day he was learning more both about his host and the customs of the day. Tonight, for example, he would observe—

It was then, on that one word, that the implications hit him.

On another level of existence, in another age, Martin was trying to stop himself reaching for the whisky bottle for the third time. The trouble with this was that it relied too much on speculation.

It was fine for Argyle to be cock-a-hoop and say it was bound to be a success. Right, it had worked with twelve cases but, like the wonder drugs that had appeared in the last decade, cures might be limited to the few.

Argyle came in as he was reaching for a drink, as usual bouncing with confidence.

"Got a lot of news for you, old son, managed to make some important contacts. First of all, I've managed to get details in respects of this stuff. In the first place the recipient goes to bed and sleeps in an outwardly normal way. He over-sleeps slightly in the morning but begins to exhibit minor symptoms as soon as he comes down."

"What kind of symptoms?" Martin was filling his glass, shakily.

"Well, first he seems withdrawn, absent-mined, does not seem to hear what is said to him. He shows no interest in his own but exhibits a flurry of activity in other matters. This symptom lasts around four days and the change is announced, or becomes apparent on the fifth day."

"The fifth day." Martin glanced at the office calendar. "That's Carnival Day."

"Eh—what?" Argyle looked blank.

"Oh don't be so bloody obtuse man, *our* Carnival for the complex only. The old man started the tradition forty years ago, Wenstone junior just carried it on. They hold it every year."

Argyle's face brightened. "Of course, I had forgotten. The day the bonuses and merit awards are presented. Everyone arrives in fancy dress, there's a grand party, a dance, all that sort of thing."

He paused and grinned. "Fits in perfectly. I have no doubt the boss will use the occasion to announce his retirement."

"I wish I felt as damn confident as you." Martin drained his glass.

"Aren't you listening to me, man? I was trying to tell you, he's showing all the symptoms. Like the others, he's ringing around all over the place, obviously making plans. He's acting out of character and, for reasons unknown, he limps occasionally. Another thing, he keeps fingering the top of his right ear and then inspecting his fingertips. I tell you, man, he's on his way out."

"Where the hell are you getting all this information?"

"I've come to an arrangement with one of his household servants."

"More money!"

"Well, of course, I've got to pay the bloody man, Martin, but, in the long run, it will get us out from under. We only need one hit and you know the opportunities which are passed up here."

"You've still got this hit-man laid on?"

"Naturally, I'd be a fool if I didn't prepare for every contingency however remote."

Adam Wenstone had a sick feeling of horror inside him. Why had he not failed to see, realized sooner? He was not going to stand aside and watch a gun fight. He was going to be a participant, he and his host, were going to be the target when the shooting started. A man called Mex—reputedly Godawful fast—going to make him his target.

His host was not happy either. He had a weary resignation concerning the future. If he came out of this alive, he was away. He'd join a wagon train to far away or just ride out— He'd go so far that no one had ever heard of Limpy and come in to challenge him with a gun. It was not from choice, he had been born here. His folks had died here when some sickness had swept the town some nine years ago.

Adam knew that his host meant it, once the man made a decision, he stuck to it although it hurt to leave his home.

Sundown, opposite the saloon, the setting sun throwing long black shadows across the road but giving advantage to neither man.

Adam admitted to himself that he was terrified. There was nothing he could *do*. He was like a fish in a bowl, swirling round and round in a desperate effort to escape and there was no escape. He accused himself also. He had been quite happy to lean back and *observe* before the implications hit him.

The bullets, if they came first and accurately, would hit *their* body, a body belonging to himself and his host.

There were no obvious spectators on the street, they were there but too experienced to show themselves. Men could miss, or agonizingly hit, let fly in a fury. Then there was the death shot—Adam would call it a reflex. Old Ma Spinney had died like that years ago, a shot from a dying man as he fell.

The Mex, when he came to meet them, was tall and sallow. He was a man who liked killing and took some pride in his appearance so that people would always recognize him and give him respect.

Adam never knew who shouted *"Draw!"* but he felt his host go for it with bewildering speed.

The Mex was faster.

Faster but less accurate.

It felt as if a red-hot poker had been slapped against Limpy's head but his own guns had already jerked in his hands.

The Mex jerked as if he had been heavily punched.

He took three uncertain steps, then he crumpled into an untidy heap. There were two large holes, almost side by side, in the center of his chest.

The conspirators had not taken the four-day wait easily. Martin needed constant resort to the bottle to keep his nerves under control.

Argyle, on the other hand, was outwardly more assured than ever. "I repeat, man, there is no mistaking the pointers, they fit in like the others all along the line."

Martin nodded almost from habit. Why couldn't he dismiss the uneasy feeling that Argyle was talking just to convince himself and that he, too, was harboring inner doubts.

He handed Martin a spare pair of binoculars. "Get a good view from up here on the balcony, see the parade as it crosses the sports fields and reaches the main hall. Hello, there's the boss's car—ah, it looks as if he's dumped that Pilgrim Father costume he usually wears. Good God! Look at that! Didn't I say, didn't I tell you!"

There was some confusion at the main gate also and the security man was becoming aggressive. "You can't bring that in here."

"Why not? I've an authority here signed by Mr. Wenstone himself."

"Not for a damn great truck. What's in it, anyway?"

"Well printed on the side is the word **HORSES**—you can read I assume?"

The security man went through his list and colored slightly. "I'm sorry, friend, I really am, but a horse—for the boss—good God!"

"So strange?"

"Hell, yes. If you handed Mr. Wenstone a horse, he'd look for a starter button. I've worked for him for years and my old man before me."

"Perhaps he just wants to lead it."

"Ah. you're probably right, he might just manage that to head the parade to the conference area."

"Yes, you're probably right."

Up on the balcony Argyle said: "There, there, I told you! Complete change, can you imagine the old Wenstone going through a charade like that? There's even a bloody horse carrier thing there, but the Boss doesn't know one end of a horse from the other."

There was trouble in the horsebox, too. Bulmer the chief groom—mainly an executive position—was having personal troubles.

"What's the trouble with that damn mare, Selby?"

"Jesse doesn't like bands, sir, I did mention it at the time. We should have brought, Mabel, nothing troubles her."

"Are you questioning my judgment, Selby? Who the hell do you think you are? If she won't move, give her a touch of the whip to help her along."

"Some trouble here?" A man walked up the ramp and into the transit.

"Get out of here, you." Bulmer loved throwing his weight around and lost his temper easily. "I've enough trouble on my hands without some idiot prancing in here dressed up as a stage cowboy. You'd like me to call security, perhaps?"

The other nodded expressionlessly. "Yes—yes, I'd rather like that. I pay his wages."

Bulmer opened his mouth to retort but no sound carne. He was not too insensitive to realize that this man had authority.

Wenstone turned to Selby. "I gather from some of the conversation that the mare is nervous."

"Yes, sir, Jesse doesn't like bands, sir, the drums and that."

"Poor old lady. Here, give her to me."

He took the bridle and began to talk to her. They could not hear what he said and the soft words he used were beyond them anyway. His hands stroked her head and neck, pulled gently at her ears. "Come on, girl, come on."

They saw him lead the animal down the ramp and onto the ground. They saw him put his foot into the stirrup and swing himself easily into the saddle.

Up on the balcony Argyle had a fixed leer of utter disbelief. "He can't ride." It no longer comforted him that Wenstone had changed.

Despite the change the man appeared, even at this distance, to have gained additional control.

Webster, a junior executive, joined them on the balcony. He carried one of the new, digital binoculars. "What do you mean, the Boss can't ride? I do a bit of riding myself and look at the way he sits the saddle. He's good, let me tell you; been riding since a kid, no doubt."

He leaned forward, pointing. "The Old West is one of my personal hobbies and that fancy dress of his is spot on, take it from me. The guns too are exactly placed for a quick draw. Obviously someone who knows his business has advised him on detail."

Argyle said nothing he had a sick feeling inside that somehow the whole business had gone sour.

Martin, for his part, was near to tears and the bottle now failed to assure him.

Turning away from the parade below, he almost collided with yet another who had joined the group. "Get out of my damned way!"

"Sorry, I can't do that. I want you and Mr. Argyle together. Mr. Wenstone wants you in his office in half an hour."

Wenstone had not bothered to change back to civilian clothes but sat on the edge of his desk, smiling inwardly with relief. God that had been close. He raised his hand, fingered his ear then studied his fingers briefly. No, he was not bleeding but he kept feeling he might be. That blasted dago had taken off the top of his ear and burned a short furrow in his scalp as well. It was an experience he had somehow brought back which was more vivid than memory.

Someone pressed the announcer plate on the outside of the door, and Wenstone said: "Come in."

Martin came first, red faced and looking close to tears. Argyle, also deflated but with a shaky smile of defiance. "I don't know what this is all about," he said. "This man here," he jerked his head at the third member of the party who entered behind them, "maybe, as he says, he's a police official but—"

"Save it." Wenstone cut him short. "We knew all about it from the beginning. Obviously we do not advertise the fact but all our financial computers are fitted with micro-surveillance units as well as our main offices. If necessary we can trace a single ancient coin round the world. We were well aware, therefore, of your incursion into high finance with our money which, needless to say, was never confirmed. Similarly we know of the odd million you paid to a professional assassin to dispose of me in case your first trick went wrong."

Wenstone withdrew one of his six-guns from its holster, inspected it and replaced it. "I would like to have disposed of you both cleanly, in fair fight with one of these but unfortunately present law does not permit it. However, I have not brought here to gloat but to tell you, before you do 'life,' exactly what your formula mystery drug did."

He paused and smiled at the third member of the party. "Oh, do sit down First Class Officer Bradley—liquor—coffee—tea—? Just press the button in the arm of your chair. However to return to the drug which, since analysis, is known as Genetic Stimulant. In short the drug awakens a racial memory so vividly that the recipient seems to revert back many generations to some outstanding event in his past. Very often it is not a good incident, perhaps a mass execution, the wholesale slaughter of the innocent and like incidents. I cannot report on all but I have the outlines of two and these two, being honorable men felt that they must redeem themselves in this life for the evils they had committed in the past. Therefore it was concluded, incorrectly, that everyone given the drug would change their life-style completely."

Wenstone paused and smiled faintly. "I was lucky, my grandfather, many times removed, was a gunman named Limpy. Not from choice, it was forced upon him and, anyway, he got out from under long before his life was over."

He paused and looked long and hard at the two accused men in turn. "I'm well aware, needless to say, that you paid a top flight hit-man over a million of the firm's money to have me removed should the drug fail. But for this there might have been mitigating circumstances; I might have spoken on your behalf. Unwittingly you did me a favor, you, gave another life, other knowledge and other senses which I had never known about before."

He shook his head, sighed and looked at Bradley, the police officer. "Can you get rid of these two?"

"Yes, sir, I've a couple of men waiting in the corridor, outside."

When they had gone, Wenstone said: "Have any trouble with the hit-man?"

"Oh, no, sir. We picked him up in the Long Corridor where he intended to wait for you."

"Oh, yes, that reminds me . . . " Wenstone crossed his office to his secretary's desk in the corner. "The photos from our surveillance cameras." He handed the other a large envelope.

"Thank you, Mr. Wenstone—er—excuse me asking, sir, but have you had an accident recently?"

"No—why?"

"You were walking with a distinct limp, sir."

Wenstone said easily: "Oh, my foot went to sleep when I was leaning on the desk."

Inwardly he cursed himself. He really must force himself to place his foot flat on the floor in a normal way.

He said: "Please tell me more about this hit-man."

"Well he offered no resistance, sir. With seven guns pointed at him, he had little choice. Needless to say, he was in fancy dress like everyone else. The odd part being he was dressed as a cowboy, just like you, although his was a darker costume than yours. He had some nasty weapons dotted around inside it, too."

"Tell me, was he tall, thin and kind of sneery?"

"Yes, sir, now that you come to mention it, he was. Do you think you might have met him at some time, sir?"

"Not really, just a mental picture in my mind."

"He was not a Nordic type, sir, more dark skinned if you understand me but, by God, he was thorough. A large part of that fancy dress costume was not fancy. The six-guns in the holster were real and fully loaded."

"Well, it is strange that." Wenstone drew his own guns and spun them deftly round his index fingers. "So are mine."

DARK PEAK

Brian Ball

"We're off to see the Bog Man," we finished, as the train drew in. "The Wonderful Bog Man of Gryse!"

There was no wonderment, though. And we did get to see what we had set out to see.

To our everlasting regret.

I was with, as they say, Melissa. Zara, our mutual friend, who was more or less settled in England now, had come along, too, all of us thinking of careers and each other, and nothing at all about the what we might chance upon in the Dark Peak.

We'd come on a none-too-serious quest for enlightenment about the past.

We'd got lightweight hiking boots on, and we'd brought the advised emergency gear, an old fashioned metal container with plasters and bandages and things, naturally a cell phone, enough food and drink, a torch, maps, all in an old rucksack I'd bought for next to nothing at a car boot sale. Myself and my lady were in shorts, me with my shirt looped round my waist, Melissa looking languorous and fit at the same time, tall and svelte.

She's black, startling so, against my white body, which is big and solid and won't tan. I just singe.

Zara's Persian, so she keeps out of the sun, an inherited trait.

She looked oriental and elegant and we all felt exhilarated as we looked up and down the one street of Grysethorpe for our starting-point, which was to see the old, very *very* old, gentleman himself.

We were all capable young people.

Melissa was going to be a teacher of infants one day, but her hobby was anthropology, hence the impulse for our trip. Zara had studied medicine in Teheran until the mullahs told her not to, hanging her father and brother to reinforce the point. She hadn't yet found a place in a medical school over here, but she had hopes that the Institute of Tropical Medicine might give her at least an interview.

We *were* off to see the Bog Man.

And where he'd been found amongst the Standing Stones, deep in the astonishing gruel of chemicals about two metres down in a peat bog, where he'd been murdered about three thousand years ago. But it had all been so wonderfully preserved, all of it, down to some shreds of vegetable and animal fiber that said he was wearing thonged sandals, leather breeches, and a wolfskin cloak, and that it could be shown to an invited few, and we were invited.

Melissa had made the enquiries, got a no, but I'd fixed that. I had my Master's in Marine Biology, but it was the genetic research that had go us tickets to the very exclusive museum that was his last resting place— I have used a term that is not wholly accurate I realise: I have to pause. *It never rested.*

I'll spell the whole, terrible tragedy out.

Only a few shards of bone belonging to two of his attackers had been preserved, as I say, but the Bog Man, in a sense, had survived.

"I suppose we'll get postcards and such from the museum?" said Melissa. "I hope they're scary. I want to send a few to my friends."

"There's a happy thought," I said. "Right, Zara? You want some? For the Ayatollas?"

"I wouldn't do that, even to them."

She's careful about her pronouncements. They have to exactly mirror her thoughts, otherwise she'd be unfaithful to her extremely demanding religion. They don't see shades of gray in thought or speech, the followers of Zoroaster.

Only black and white.

Good and Evil.

"He's just joking," said Melissa. "Anyway, my friends will go for this wolfskin cloak he was in. Cooky. Yes?"

"Oh, you, Melissa!" Zara said fondly. She looked content rather than happy. That is, until we asked for directions to the small museum where they kept the Bog Man, please.

There's usually a direction post to such institutions even in small towns, but not in the charming small town—village, really—of Grysethorpe.

"Where is it, my dears?" said the center one of the three middle aged women in Barbour wellies, overtight jeans and tank tops that didn't suit them, all with blondish streaked hair with a touch of gray, all very confident of themselves, this one with the cut-glass voice of the finishing schools.

Melissa explained the purpose of our quest.

"Oh, you've been *invited!*" said left flank, bright red tank top and a coral necklace.

"So pleased you've come to visit," said right flank, flashing the big sapphire on her second finger.

The center woman, making decisions, said, "We'll take you there. And where are you three darlings from?"

Darlings.

All three of them were alert.

How could we know that these frightful hags would have such a devastating impact on our three young lives? But we sensed something, all of us.

Why should they wish to know anything at all about us?

Their gaze was concentrated, the three sets of eyes, on Zara. Did they sense her psychic and very special aura?

"From somewhere Mid Eastern?" suggested right flank silkily to Zara. "Lovely textures. Beautiful patterns. And a short sari sort of thing, too. Ducky!"

Zara wouldn't answer.

"Oh, shy!" said left flank heartily. "I like modesty in a young woman. And you, dear?"

"Fulham," said Melissa.

"Really? It must be very interesting for you!"

"Ooo, isn't it just?" yowled Melissa lasciviously, quite able to deflect intrusive questions. "Ooo, you should be there!"

The leader looked a question at me.

"Sheffield," I said politely.

"Well, you're a big, big Steeler, aren't you?" said left flank, bulging over turquoise and fluorescent yellow. "I suppose you play rugby rather violently?"

"Soccer. And cricket."

"Oh, how simply ambidextrous of you!" right flank said.

"I like to boot things hard in winter. And hit them hard in summer."

She smiled, and I found myself wondering about her teeth. Was there a certain curl to the incisors when she laughed aloud at my discomfiture?

"Hit things hard!" repeated right flank laughing aloud, not a pleasant laugh.

"Not us, please!" encored left flank.

Zara had quite turned her face away from them.

I thought I heard a whisper from her, an ancient incantation to keep secure what primeval man could keep faith with.

Air, Fire, Water, Stone.

Just keep it to the four elements we know well. We can live with those. And, we implore you, don't let the very ground give up its secrets.

"You'll be sure to see the Stones!" called the leader of the small pack, as she left us at the imposing entrance to the museum. It had been an early nineteenth century Primitive Methodist chapel in the local handsome dark stone.

I felt myself approving. They'd recycled it. Not religion any more, but a shrine nevertheless.

"Yes, isn't it?" said the young man who told me he was so glad to see us after he'd carefully inspected the letter the society had sent me. "I'm Mr. Atkinson."

"I have seen enough," Zara said. "I will wait outside."

"Zara?"

"I need fresh air, Ben."

The lighting showed the powerful features of the face, the thickness of the fingers, the frayed texture of the shreds of wolf skin cloak, and the way the thongs of the sandals had lapped their way up almost to the bones of the thick knees.

That bronze spear point in his back!

Had he howled his rage to the forested hills?

"Some guy?" asked Melissa. ""I wasn't expecting the size."

Mr Atkinson offered help.

"Two metres wasn't unusual then," he said. "If you got past infancy, you had a good chance of growing to a full height, and we know that lots of the men were much bigger than the present European average. Only the strong survived."

"He didn't," I found myself saying.

"Ah? I know that some of our more sensitive, or rather vulnerable, visitors can get a nasty turn just by one look at Our Harry— oh, shouldn't have said that! Sorry!"

Melissa and I were both curious.

We enquired about the name and we got an explanation. Someone on the committee had proposed it, and since calling the mummified corpse just The Bog Man seemed a bit callous, then Harry it was. It became *Ours*.

Our Harry.

Just the kind of bloke you'd come across down at the pub.

No. In a darker location altogether.

"Our Harry it is, then," said Melissa. "I see a Mr. Julius Fisk spent years on the dig. He isn't on the committee, I see?"

You'd have thought he'd have been on the committee, but he wasn't, according to the details we scanned in the pamphlet we bought from Atkinson.

Melissa asked about this.

"Well, it's difficult," said the Curator. "You see, it was private property, and at the time of Mr Fisk's discovery, there was no right of public access. Yes, yes," he said, forestalling our further questions. He glibly explained that Julius Fisk was, after all, an *amateur*, whereas the Foundation took its responsibilities very seriously and completely *professionally*.

And no, they were out of postcards. The reprint could take a week or two.

"Poor old Fisk got zilch, then, Mr Atkinson?"

"Leave it," hissed Melissa.

I looked at my watch. An hour had passed.

"Zara!"

"I bought an ice-cream," she said. "The van comes for a few minutes every day about this time, then it goes. I talked to the boy who drives it. He's from Albania. He doesn't like England."

"We go this way, Zara," said Melissa.

She's the pathfinder.

"You sure you wouldn't prefer us all just to turn round and get on one of those slow trains back to Sheffield? Reggae and peppered chicken, maybe yams and hot chilli sauce, at Josh's?"

This was a newish, spare-looking place a mile out of the center, with good food and good music, bring your own beer, wine if you preferred.

Nothing hard, and no drugs, please. Josh was a short, burly, dreadlocked man who knew how to run a place. I think he'd looked Zara over with approval the last time we'd been there together.

"You're nice," said Zara, leading the way up the winding track just past the church. "We'll go on."

I handed her my pack and got my shirt on. She gave me the pack back. There's a touch of the aristocrat about her.

Was.

"Onwards and upwards!"

"To the Stones," said Melissa, doubtfully, I thought at the time.

"It's not a good time to be out in the dark," came a voice seemingly from nowhere, a cracked, old man's voice, too.

We were alongside the graveyard.

Melissa screamed.

"Oh, my god!" Zara hung onto my arm.

Then we saw him.

He'd been in deep shadow. There was a huge old yew with thick densely-leaved branches, and because we'd had the sun slanting in our eyes, he'd been invisible to us. He advanced on Zara.

"I said it's not a good time to be out in the dark for your kind."

He was alone, an old, tall, thin creature, with legs like sticks and a green pack on his back and eyeglasses as thick as an old-fashioned beer bottle's base.

The Iranian girl who would have it that she was Persian wanted to talk to the spidery old man. It surprised me, for she had been badly shaken by the creaky warning from of the gloom.

"Sir?"

"You should know," he told her. "Your kind do."

I didn't like that, and he saw it.

"You think I have something against foreigners? Those of a different faith? Those who know the old ways?"

Melissa got between us.

"Sir? We apologise."

"But they're just stones," I said.

Well, *the* Stones.

Stones.

Twenty-one bits of rock.

"I say no more, but I think this young lady understands," he told us, and

I for one was glad to see the back of him.

"Ben. Let's move."

"O.K."

Ahead was a bleak landscape, made bleaker by the way the last of the sun's rays, which were golden-brown, with some crimson amongst low cloud, shone where the sheep had cropped what they could of the tufts of strong grasses.

The slanting sunlight enhanced its glow.

We made good time, and about forty minutes after the spidery-legged old man's warning, we got our first look into the cleft in the dark rock where the stones had been erected.

The Stones were weathered.

All except one.

"—eighteen, nineteen, twenty and one. And another!"

Melissa checked the pamphlet we'd bought at the museum.

"Someone's miscounted," I said.

"Odd," said Melissa.

"Twenty-two," confirmed Zara.

"But it's not a Standing Stone. It's sort of leaning against the rocks. Doesn't count," I said.

I checked again.

"This one's older rock," I said.

"Here, Melissa. Look. And you, Zara."

"No thanks," I got from Zara.

I felt a rising of excitement. The leaning rock was a few metres from a cave.

"I wonder how far it goes into the rock. I'll have a look."

"Don't, please, Ben. It isn't safe. Any shorings will have longs since rotted away. You can get a roof fall at any time. It's an opening for the miners. Tin, maybe. Silver, probably. They all worked it, going back to the Phoenicians. They all used slave labor."

"So why the extra stone?" I said. "Twenty-one we should have, now one more. So, why?"

The sun was down, and I could see that Zara was shivering.

"What did that old guy mean, Zara? You know, down at the church."

I had pondered the matter. He hadn't intentionally offended any of us. I knew that now.

Your kind?

The old ways?

I knew that her religion was incredibly ancient. The Persians had learned from their predecessors, the Avestans, and no one could quite put a date on their times. They had given the Persians the names of the twin and opposing forces, but at the time I couldn't recall the names Zara had told me about.

And, clearly, this wasn't the proper moment to question her.

"Please? May we leave it?"

I wanted to, but Melissa had become interested.

"Is it something to do with your beliefs, Zara?"

A heavy cloud was beginning to obscure the last of the red glow over the peaks. Zara hadn't answered Melissa. We were in a bad time. We all knew it.

And then, just like that, the mist came down, but it was a swirling, mote-filled mist, more of a—*miasma*. It was as though the air itself had been taken away from us.

Air.

"Ben?" said Melissa quietly.

Zara said something in her own language, but I couldn't make out the syllables sufficiently well to give a form to the word. And when she repeated it, all I got was something like, "A-ry-man!"

"It's getting darker," muttered Melissa.

"A miasmic mist," I said. "That's all. We're in a deep little ravine, so it's bound to be darker down here."

We all heard the howls at the same time. For my part, I had just hefted the packed rucksack onto my back, and I was still in an odd state in which I couldn't make up my mind as to whether we were under threat or not.

We were.

"What's that?" said Melissa. "Dogs? Someone's dogs out there?"

The mist was colder, the light had almost gone.

"I suppose someone's walking their dogs, but it's late for that kind of thing. Maybe a couple of pets have got lost."

"Not pets," said Zara.

In the last of the dying light, I could see her face set in a stone-like gaze. I listened.

It wasn't a canine howl, no. Zara was right.

"We should move. Now!"

"Yes. Come on."

But we had lost our sense of direction. The freezing mist had disoriented us.

"Ben!" cried Melissa.

I tripped and fell, my hands steadied by a rotting log that only served to make the impact against a stone outcrop all the worse. Consciousness left me as I cracked my head against the gritty stone. I heard Melissa's cry, probably after only two or three seconds of oblivion.

I saw torches in the darkness, and I glimpsed the faces of Furies.

"Ben!" screamed Melissa. "It's those cursed bitches from the town!"

Bitches?

From the town?

They came out of the miasma, white and fat and naked, ten, a dozen, maybe more, bright red flares smoked and burned and revealed the bizarrely contorted faces of the women.

They were feral creatures.

I was hidden from their view, I realised.

The fallen log was part of a small barrier of rotted timbers, and the stone outcrop on which I had damaged my head gave additional cover. I was grateful for it,

"Ahriman!" I heard three or four yell, almost in unison.

"He will come!"

"We've got the Persian bitch!"

Persian, I said silently. *Not* Iranian. So they knew something at least of Zara's origins.

Then I knew: Zara had shrieked, in that strange oriental way, the name of the evil being, the one implacably opposed to the forces of good.

Ahriman.

Melissa's despairing scream rocked me to the core of my being.

"Ben! Come to me!"

Triumphant calls came from the miasmic gloom.

"We've got the Fulham bitch, too. She's hiding in the pit!"

"Then roll the stone down on her. We'll keep her for later!"

The last was an instruction that was answered immediately by two or three of the hags. It was the leader again.

I reasoned some of it out in that instant. Twenty-two stones, where there should be twenty-one.

A pit?

A stone lying by a pit?

I hadn't seen a pit, but we had found the entrance to one of the ancient diggings, hadn't we? Was that their *pit?*

That was as far as I got, for I risked a glance and saw that the snarling leader, torch held high to try to penetrate the awful gloom, was carrying in her right hand a gleaming hatchet.

My thoughts were clearing. I had some of it worked out.

Pit. Silver. A pre-Roman site. Bronze weapons.

A very old civilisation.

"He's here. Close by."

I saw the flash of a sapphire ring.

Right flank.

A vivid red: a coral necklace.

Left flank.

"He won't get far," the leader said, regaining some measure of control. "Ahriman comes!"

It was long past time for me to do my part. I felt the flow of blood through my arms and legs. My strength was returning. I got to my feet and drove myself forward. A break in the mist showed me a terrible sight.

The Stones were the background to an evil that should not exist in the Dark Peak, but which was there before my staring eyes. Zara was naked.

She was quite alone, ringed by a pack of Harpies, all brandishing torches and all too carried away by their blood-lust to note my emergence from my hiding-place.

The cry was loudest from the leader of the hags.

"—-riman, Come!"

The hag-bitch thrust her left hand out, almost into Zara's long, black hair.

Then Zara moved.

She reached for the flare.

She called on the force of light, the Zoroastrian twin and opposing deity.

"Ozmud!"

"Ahriman!" shrieked the bitch-hag.

She reached to her burned eyes, dropping the hatchet and yelling in appalled rage at the Persian woman who had blinded her.

I felt the blow halfway up my back.

I knew what it was. The spear point was in my spine. A violent event from three millennia ago was being repeated. I was down again, my head crashing against something hard. I fell into water.

I had been concussed before, hurt badly. Not like this.

What could I do?

I tumbled, fell and sank into water and oblivion.

Josh could forget his hopes of Zara, for I heard the terrible noises that spoke of the manner of her death.

She got—

There is a word that is not often used, but pathologists know it: they have to deal with the aftermath. It is *rended.*

Then I felt the weight of the rucksack. It wasn't much of a burden. I thought to throw it off before I went in pursuit of my own form of vengeance.

The spear lay beside me, the point embedded in both the cell-phone and the strong metal casing of the first aid box. Those, and the thickness of heavy-duty, old-fashioned canvas had saved me.

"Move," I grunted, and leapt towards the hellish circle and the *thing* that was throwing body parts to them.

"Ahriman!" they screamed.

Our Harry.

Of course.

That was their utterly sick and contemptuous way of giving the awakened devil a harmless, old-fashioned name. The kind of bloke you met—

"Zara!" I roared.

I hefted the spear: I can throw things hard, javelins, shot, and cricket balls, whatever is needed.

It should have hit him square in the throat, but this thing at one time had been a warrior.

Slave master or mine owner?

Escapee or pursuer, himself to be pursued and hunted to a cold death in a deep bog that would turn to peat and mummify him— *it!*

He eased aside, and the spear thudded into the tufted grass a foot from his right. Then he was up and drawing a long, heavy knife from a skin scabbard, a hunter in the lead, and a pack of hell hags screeching in his wake. They left the fighting to their grim champion.

I ran at him, arms outstretched to rip his glaring eyes from his bearded, shaggy head, and his head from his shoulders, then tear him apart and send him back into the mists of time. I think he could have killed me within two seconds. But I would have marked him, torn some part of his long-dead corpse away, an arm, maybe, a leg if I could tangle with him.

We were near to clashing, when a hand feebly grasped my ankle and momentarily checked me. I swung aside from the beast's charge and the blinded leader of the hags swung at me with a glittering edged weapon in her free hand. She sobbed her loyalty to it.

I put my shoulder down and caught it in a fierce grinding of bone and muscle.

Then we were on the ground, rolling in the bracken and grass, the thing stabbing and yelling, its breath reeking of the charnel house, its long, bloodied incisors searching to tear out my jugular vein. I am strong, but this *thing* had iron tendons and stone bones. Its weight was more than mine, and its ferocity outmatched anything that even the fear of death could bring me to.

I reached out a hand to ward off the flint knife.

I rolled away in a free moment.

The hags screamed in triumph.

The leader yelled in pain.

My hand felt a long, smooth handle.

Hatchet.

Edged weapon.

Hers.

I swung, harder than I have ever swung at anything.

The blade sank deep into the iron tendons, cutting through gore-matted beard and hair, slicing easily into the thick veins of the neck, and only half-stopping at the intersection of skull and vertebrae.

The Bog Man's mouth opened. I saw the fangs.

It tried to roar. Then it dropped the flint knife and instinctively raised both hands to the throat.

"Die again!"

I swung, just as hard, and the thing's head rocked on the torso and then fell away into the smoke and mist. The twice-dead headless corpse remained upright for a moment, and then it slowly toppled away, to fall at the feet of the hag who had tried to slice my belly open. I held still in shock.

She must have had some partial sight, for she reached out to the thing and placed her head at the pumping junction where head and body should have been.

What was she doing?

I reeled. I was almost exhausted. I was back in my place, one with the rest of humanity. But the hag bitch's cautious movements held me in a spell. Simply, I couldn't do the things that needed my attention.

What was she doing now?

She reached into the grass in what seemed to be almost tender carefulness, then her hands discovered the thing's head. She reached for it, held it in her two large hands and then crushed it to her bloodied breasts in a wild protective movement, as if she could comfort the *thing* and restore it to some form of life.

She keened over the head for a second or two.

Then I recovered my wits. I could do nothing for poor, infinitely courageous Zara, but I could rescue my woman.

"Kill!" screamed back the hag pack.

"Stones!" shrieked the burned woman. "Stone him!"

I half-raised the edged weapon. I could kill some of them, wound more. But there was a pack of them, and they held pieces of grit stone in their hands. I heard a call as they armed themselves.

Melissa!

"Melissa!" I called back, but my voice was without power.

"In the cave!"

The first flight of stones was badly aimed. One glanced off my left shoulder. It hurt and helped at the same time. These were not ordinary upper class Englishwomen. They were ghouls.

But could I leave Melissa under the Stone?

No.

Never.

It was, then, a fight to the death. Against a shower of heavy stones, I must soon be knocked down. How many could I kill by a berserker charge?

Not enough.

And then came a colossal blast of sound that had us all confounded. It was the unmistakable roar of a modern, heavy weapon. It filled the valley and left a ringing silence. And it had stopped the women in their tracks. Rocks fell from their nerveless hands. Like me, they knew the sound of a shotgun's blast.

"This is a repeating shotgun," called a reedy, old man's voice. "I have six rounds left, and a belt of ammunition on my shoulder!"

"Fisk!" hissed the half-blinded woman.

"You will all go now!"

"Never!" she shrieked back.

For answer, he blasted the headless torso lying beside her.

"You die, Fisk!" she screamed.

"Leave the head!"

Another blast of sound filled the ravine.

The head rolled away. I saw its fangs for the last time.

Fisk knew what to do, and in a matter of three or four minutes we had prised the twenty-second out. Melissa choked, spat dust out and told me that she was never again going to let me out of her sight, if she could help it.

The rest of it was difficult.

"Zara? No!"

She didn't want to believe it. She was traumatised. But we helped one another down into the town and then collapsed. Fisk turned to us:

"Forget tonight. All of it. For your very souls' sake! Say nothing! They will know!"

I got delayed concussion. That's how the paramedics found me. I was unconscious for the next thirty-six hours. I asked for Melissa and Zara. One traumatised and with her parents in Fulham. Regretfully, one mauled to death. Then, a calm Divisional Superintendent of police came to take my statement at the hospital.

"Really sir, A dozen naked women? Shotguns and spears? A savage, you say, sir? I'll let you recover. I'll come back. You rest, sir."

I was a hero and the medical staff regarded me with some awe. In the press, none of it had happened as we had experienced it.

The detective came back after I had been sedated for half a day.

"Fisk? He was there! Without him, we'd all be dead!"

"We're all truly sorry about Mr Julius Fisk, sir. He had a heart attack only yesterday. Fatal, I'm afraid. You ready to make a— well, a proper statement now you've rested, sir?"

For your very souls' sake!

"Accusations of murder?" he said. "That, sir, is the most serious matter of all. But our Scene of Crime Officers have already been over the ground most carefully. And I can assure you that what had emerged has been exactly what was first reported in the newspapers. We found evidence of a terrible assault and mutilation, yes, but it was clear that the marauding large cat killed the young lady. We found it headless, and the creature's head nearby. Ferocious beast! It's been marauding in these parts for over a year. Took very many sheep, and threatened the lives of more than one child. You're a brave young man."

"Puma? It was the damned Bog Man!"

"Sir, let's be reasonable. We are all most grateful to you."

They gave me sedatives again and I blacked out for two more days. Melissa came to see me.

"Sorry," she said. "I had a sort of breakdown. My dad came for me."

"But you're back."

"Forever, Ben. Don't talk about it now. Let's go home."

"What do we do?" I said. "Newspapers? Television? Channel Five?"

For your very souls' sake!

But Zara needed to be avenged!

I asked Melissa to corroborate my story.

"They won't believe us, Ben."

"Someone has to!"

We set out our story for the media. *Sorry.*

Our story of wild naked middle-aged women was not even considered seriously by them. Were we looking for a payout? That was their view: that we had further sensationalised a truly ghastly killing, dressing it up with rumors and legends and a bit of archaeological evidence. The police had given them all the facts they wanted, and no thanks.

And there would be no payouts, of course.

I gave it three days and went back to Grysethorpe.

Melissa said she couldn't take any more. Three distant cousins of Zara's had turned up from Paris and angrily told me they didn't want any more stories about her. They would see that she was cared for properly when her body was released after the inquest. They treated us with some suspicion and left.

For your very souls' sake!

No. I had to go on.

It was raining when I got off the train at the tidy station. The wind hit me in the face as I walked along the only street and turned the corner as were three had on that fateful day.

I was unsurprised to see that the place was boarded up. A neat notice informed visitors that the place was closed so that repairs could be carried out. I banged on the door and called for Fisk. There was no answer. I looked through the windows at street level, but they had been fitted with drapes where they were not covered in heavy-duty boarding. I looked up to a small window just below the stone arch of the old chapel.

And I saw her.

It was the leader of the hags.

It was just a glimpse, but I have keen eyes and I know that in that single instant she recognised me. The face was badly scarred, and there was just one glittering eye to glare at me. I backed away, appalled.

"A burned lady with one eye, sir?" asked Gryesthorpe's only policeman at the police house. "That must be Lady Seymour-Fitzgerald, sir. Very good family. Friends of the Lord Lieutenant. Distressing accident. Bad thing, that."

"I saw them. Her."

He believed me! But he was local, so he would know of the damned hell-hags. "I never recommend these gas cylinder barbecue kits. Blow up. And blow up it did, the poor lady."

It was a cover up. It had been from the start.

They'd found a puma, and cut its head off.

"Like to have a photograph of the head, sir? You have a good eye with an axe, I'll say that. But I gather you're a cricketer? Two nice cuts to mid off, those!"

"How about the axe?"

He told me.

"Boy Scouts camp near here, you see, and someone got careless and they lost a hatchet cutting woodfalls near the Stones. We'll keep it as evidence for a while. Anything else, sir?"

"About Mr. Julius Fisk."

"Thought the Super had told you, sir. Heart attack, it was. You all right, sir?"

"I see the museum's undergoing repairs."

"Vandals, that. We don't get many here. I see to that! But Mr. Atkinson couldn't take it and left."

He was in the cover up. I could do no more.

I got Fisk's letter the next day. It arrived by hand courtesy of his housekeeper. She said she should really have given it to the police, but it had been his wish that I be found and receive it. At the hospital they'd been sympathetic and since I was such a hero they'd bend the rules a bit and forward Fisk's letter to me. It wasn't long. I won't give anything but the gist of it.

It was a cult thing.

In pointless lives ancient desires had stirred in their heavy bosoms and ponderous bellies. Primeval thrills had suffused them. But don't underestimate their powers. And don't be too surprised if I'm not around for much longer.

72

They'd sniffed out Zara and her beliefs. Her beliefs were diametrically opposed to the strange creature they could revive at intervals. Probably, said Fisk, he had been a shaman from the area known as Mesopotamia: they thought of the god as a diabolical creature who could come back and take over the remains of one of his followers. The hags had not been able to resist this summons.

And, always, they needed blood.

Fisk's letter ended succinctly: 'Go. Now. As far as you can.'

The postcard was unsigned:

'We look forward to seeing you two.'

I knew that when I got the postcard and saw the frightful picture.

It was the Bog Man. He was in his crypt at the museum. The head was totally detached from the torso.

Melissa shrieked.

The post also had the hoped-for letter from Marine Gendives, based at Cairns. Would I undertake some work on a two-year contract that involved diving on the Reef, and could I come soon? Liked your work on the mollusc genome. Come on, mate.

"Get a visa from Australia House," I told Melissa. "You've still got student status. We can be on a plane in two days."

The phone rang. We looked at one another.

"I'll take it," I said.

"How nice you're still with us," came that familiar ice-glass voice, that of the leader of the hags.

Melissa caught the tones.

"Pack," I told her. "Five minutes and we're out."

"Zara?"

"We'll always remember her."

"Us?"

"Together."

"Them?"

"It's a new world. We'll leave this one behind."

The phone rang again. We left it.

For your very souls' sake.

Ours.

STRANGER IN OUR MIDST

John Russell Fearn

CHAPTER ONE

Meteorites?

Glenda Carlyle swept into the news editor's office and slammed the door behind her emphatically.

The frosted glass in the upper half shivered but did not break. It had been subjected to such treatment before.

"Look here, boss, what do you think I am?" she demanded, striding towards the desk where the news editor sat in shirtsleeves, busy with his blue pencil.

"Any time you smash that door glass you'll pay for it," he said, without glancing up.

"You don't expect me to come in like a lamb when you give me an assignment right off my beat, do you?"

"I never expect you to come in like a lamb, m'dear. It just isn't in you."

The news editor sat back in his swivel chair. He was a big man, square-faced, blond-haired, kindly somehow despite the arrogance he needed for his job.

"Meteorites!" Glenda exclaimed in disgust. "Meteorites!"

The news editor appraised her rounded curves for a moment and then grinned with good humor. Glenda was twenty-five, auburn-headed, pleasant but not particularly good-looking. Her approach to things and people was that of a girl who has been forced to chisel her own way through life.

"What did you find on that assignment, Glenny?"

"Old iron!"

"How much old iron? You've been in this game long enough to know that even old iron can have a human angle. This meteorite shower is worth reporting because it wasn't just one flash of light over the sky, but a deluge of lights! This being January it isn't the time for meteorites. Or, so I'm told. I'm no astronomer."

"It's never time for meteorites!" Glenda retorted, and her violet eyes—unusual with her hair coloring—glinted.

"To take a look at those still smoking chunks of iron I walked up to my knees in mud through the Sussex fields, ruined a pair of nylons, and saw nothing but a scrap-heap when I'd finished. What kind of a job is that for a girl?"

"You're not a girl, my dear; you're a reporter."

"I'm a *woman's correspondent*, and don't you forget it!"

"All right, woman's correspondent. I gave you an assignment and you fulfilled it. Let's have your copy."

Glenda tossed her story on the desk and turned to go, but the news editor's voice stopped her when she had reached the door.

"Were you dreaming when you wrote this?" he demanded. "Who the hell ever heard of a meteorite with rivets in it?"

"That's what I saw, and the *Clarion* always prints the truth—I hope. Work it out for yourself, boss."

"Okay, m'dear, thanks for handling this."

Glenda glanced up at the clock. "Half-past ten. Mind very much if I go home to bed?"

"You can go home and die for all I care. You don't count any more than the rest of us."

"'Night," Glenda said coldly, and departed.

She bade the night-staff farewell and left the building. The January night was unusually mild. She descended the steps of the *Clarion* building and walked along the street; then she turned into a quiet alley which would lead her eventually out into Holborn, crossing which thoroughfare she would again plunge into narrow ways leading through to Bloomsbury, where she occupied a small flat.

The shortcut was a mile long—a twining remnant of the past, passing between darkly looming buildings. Lights were intermittent and widely spaced, casting no more than the faintest of yellow gleams.

Suddenly a dim figure loomed ahead: the vague silhouette of a man with lumpy shoulders. He appeared to be wearing a ragged overcoat and cap. There was something about him that made Glenda stop dead, her fingers clenched about her handbag. It was full of various articles and at a pinch might be able to inflict a blow, depending on where it landed.

"Got the time, miss?" the man enquired, pausing, and his voice was coarse and brutal.

"About a quarter-to-eleven," Glenda replied jerkily, and prepared to move on. She had not covered two paces before a crushing grip on her arm swung her around.

"Y'don't know me, do yuh?" the man demanded.

"No, and I certainly don't want to!" Glenda struggled savagely and futilely to free herself, dropping her handbag in the process. "Let go of me!"

"I've waited too long t'think o' lettin' yuh go now, miss! I've watched yuh come through this alley many a night, an' I got ter thinkin' what a nice figure yuh cut as yuh go past—Then I said to meself why just let yuh go past? Why not get t'know yuh better?"

Glenda gave a mighty wrench and, her handbag forgotten, she dived desperately down the alley, coming swiftly into the radius of one of the dully glimmering-lamps.

The man reached her, twisting her about savagely. She struck out with her fists, gouged with her nails, kicked at her attacker's shins. Then to her surprise he released her so suddenly that, straining backwards as she was, she sat down with a thump.

She remained where she was, staring up in the dim light. Without warning or sound another figure had appeared—that of a tall man in a dark overcoat and soft black hat. He had his back to Glenda and stood motionless. The display of fisticuffs she had expected did not materialize.

Instead the ruffian stood staring, utterly cowed. He backed, and went on backing, and at last he turned and ran. When he had almost disappeared there came from him the strangest scream, half human and half animal. Then he reeled out of view.

The stranger turned, picked up Glenda's handbag, then reached down a hand to her elbow and gently raised her. She judged him to be about six feet in height. He was quietly dressed, his face a fathomless white in which two dark eyes gleamed in the lamplight.

"Th—thanks," Glenda said shakily, dusting herself. "You came just in time. I can never be grateful enough."

"I am only too pleased to help you." His voice was quiet and mellow, yet it had a curious inflection. It was not exactly foreign: it was too precise, as though he had consciously learned every word, and was resolved upon giving it its full meaning.

"Lucky you came this way," Glenda said.

"You think it was pure chance, then? Well, perhaps."

Glenda hugged her handbag to her, and looked at the stranger curiously.

"I'm Glenda Carlyle, and I'm on the staff of the *Clarion*."

"I see. I'm—er—Thomas Smith. Doesn't take much remembering, does it? Very plebeian."

"Yes. Yes, very."

Glenda could not understand why, but she felt uncomfortable. The manner of her rescuer was curiously unnerving. She tried to see his face more clearly but the light was too dim.

"That creature was bigger than you," she said presently, "and yet he ran for it without your laying a finger on him. What did you do? Make faces at him?"

"Perhaps," the stranger smiled.

"He screamed horribly!" Glenda added, and gave a little shiver. "I never heard a human being scream like that before. It sounded like a dog being run over. I'll never forget it."

"At root a human being is little more than an animal," Thomas Smith commented. "And that type of human being particularly so— I hope, Miss Carlyle, you will permit me to escort you home? I wouldn't feel comfortable about you otherwise."

"You're very kind, Mister Smith, but I'm sure there is no need—"

"Tell me," he interrupted, "are you afraid of me?"

"After you saved me from that—that brute, how could I be?"

"Then why don't you wish me to complete my mission by seeing you safely home?"

"I just don't want to bother you, that's all."

"No bother, believe me. Besides, I'd like to talk to you. You are an intelligent young woman and that in itself is sufficient reason for my wanting to know you better."

"Is it? Well, thanks very much. I suppose I could be attacked again, so—"

"Where do you live?"

"Bloomsbury."

"Is that far from here?"

"You're a stranger to London, then?" Glenda commented.

"Yes, Miss Carlyle. That is why I wish to talk to you. It is somewhat awkward when you are not familiar with the—place you're in."

Glenda nodded. There was some peculiarity about the way this quiet-spoken man phrased his sentences. She began walking with him at her side.

"London is quite a remarkable place," he commented, as they neared the end of the alley.

"Sprawling, dirty, and powerful," Glenda summed up. "I don't like it much myself. I was brought up in the country."

"Then you don't do the job for which you are best fitted?"

She laughed. "Do any of us?"

"You haven't answered the question," he reminded her, and with surprise she noticed the quiet, inescapable note of authority that had suddenly come into his voice.

"It's beyond answering, isn't it? I don't suppose one in a thousand of us does the job for which he or she feels best fitted. Just the way of things."

"Queer, Miss Carlyle. Very queer."

"Life's queer from the moment you're born," Glenda sighed; then she added: "And what do you do for a living, Mister Smith?"

"Oh—I'm a writer."

"And never been in London before?"

Thomas Smith did not answer the question. He and Glenda had come on to Holborn with its traffic and bright lights, and now she could see the stranger's face in detail. His nose was sharply hooked, his eyes dark, his complexion white ivory. He had high cheekbones and the line of his jaw was strongly marked and purposeful. Under the edges of his hat black hair showed.

"You're an extraordinary man with an ordinary name," Glenda told him, smiling, as she led the way to the bus stop. "Do you mind my saying that?"

"Why should I?"

"You have a habit, too, of answering a question with a question," she reminded him, and he shrugged.

"I'm sorry. I'm just naturally curious about everything—and everybody."

"I honestly don't need to trouble you any further. I'll be quite safe from here on. By comparison the streets here are quite wide and bright!"

"No doubt, but if you'll forgive me I'd much rather finish my task properly. I'm interested in seeing how you live."

"What do you expect to find unusual in the way I live?"

"Nothing—nothing at all. I'm just interested." The stranger, influenced by the direction in which Glenda was facing began to move westward along Holborn and, as is so often the way, in order to avoid explanation, Glenda dropped into step beside him letting Red Lion Street and the other turnings that would have taken her through to Bloomsbury remain out of reckoning. At the corner of Southampton Row she came to a halt: having missed the short-cuts, she felt it wiser to ride through to Euston Road, and then walk the short distance back again.

A number sixty-eight 'bus stopped. Smith followed her, and paused beside just inside the door.

"Fares, please!" intoned the driver impatiently.

Thomas Smith stood on the platform regardless. Glenda gave him a glance of surprise and then began fumbling in her handbag. He moved aside and watched her actions, then gazed at the driver.

"You two fallen out, mate?" the driver asked, and Thomas Smith looked puzzled.

"Fallen out? No. We've just got in."

"Oh, the smart set, huh? When me and my missus fall out we do it properly, and I won't even pay her 'bus fares. This smells like the same sort of thing to me."

"Does it? How interesting!"

The driver stared and then gave Glenda two tickets as she stated a destination and handed over double fare.

"Mister Smith," she said quietly, "you were gallant enough to rescue me from that tramp, and yet you are unmannerly enough to let me pay fares for both of us. Don't mind my asking, but what kind of a man are you?"

"Apparently a forgetful one," he apologized. "I had quite overlooked the fact that one must pay to travel on this—vehicle."

"You mean they don't have 'buses where you've come from? What part of the backwoods have you been in anyway?"

"Quite a distance from here, Miss Carlyle. Certainly there are no 'buses; as you call them."

"As I call them? Doesn't everybody call them that?" Glenda sat back, her violet eyes wide. "I can only make one guess about you, and it is that you have been abroad for a very long time: maybe collecting material for your writings in the Amazonian forest or somewhere, and have forgotten civilized ways."

"That might explain it," he agreed.

"But if you have been in the tropics, you ought to be sunburned, and you're not. I've never seen skin so white."

"I don't sunburn very easily."

Glenda sank back, her brows knitted. Thomas Smith remained silent too. Then Glenda stirred again.

"I've been trying to think," she said. "I can't remember having seen any of your books under the name of Thomas Smith."

"I think my writings may have been too obscure for you to have noticed them. They have been entirely historical, that is to say recorded impressions and so on. I don't give myself a name—just a number. J-N-four-seven-six. I suppose the numerals four-seven-six make sense to you?"

"Yes, I think I can manage those," Glenda agreed dryly. "Would you think me unladylike if I asked how old you are?"

"I'm a year older than you, Miss Carlyle."

"But I haven't told you my age!"

"You are twenty-five, are you not?"

"Correct." Silence again. Glenda sat gazing fixedly and Thomas Smith smiled: then the 'bus reached the stop and she and Thomas Smith were soon walking through the tree-shaded squares.

"For the life of me," Glenda said, "I can't make out how you know my age. It's uncanny! Like thought-reading!"

"You'll be twenty-six on Tuesday, next week," Thomas Smith added.

"That's right too, but how did you know?"

"I hope I may be able to commemorate the occasion in some way," he responded evasively. "You like flowers, jewelry, and you need a laptop, I believe, for that novel you're trying to write."

"Glenda halted. "Now look here, Mister Smith! How did you ever know about my wanting a laptop? That was my secret and I've never mentioned it to a soul."

"Maybe I'm psychic," Thomas suggested. "Anyhow, since you want a machine you shall have it. Don't concern yourself as to how I knew you wanted one. It was just—"

"One of those things?" Glenda suggested sarcastically.

"Maybe."

They paused before a massive Georgian residence, rounded pillars supporting the portico over the polished green front door.

"This is where I live," Glenda explained.

"Indeed? Quite a big place."

"You don't suppose I meant all of it, surely? Not on my salary! I've a small flat on the fourth floor."

"I'd like to see it."

"Well—er—some other time perhaps."

Thomas Smith smiled in his ghostly fashion. "When I said I was interested in seeing how you live, I meant it."

"I don't doubt that for a moment, but I couldn't ask you up to my flat. It would make people think."

"Why?"

Glenda gestured helplessly. "Really, Mister Smith, you re pressing your advantage too far! You may be out of touch with civilization through your having been away, but you must know that some things are not done—by nice people at least."

"But I want to see how yon live."

Before Glenda could stop him, Thomas Smith had brushed past her and turned the knob of the green door that opened onto a softly-lighted hall. The stranger gave one glance about him and then led the way up the stairs, Glenda following him swiftly, pulling at the tails of his coat and speaking in an urgent whisper.

"Mister Smith, for heavens' sake, please leave!"

He took no notice. Gaining the fourth floor he stood and waited for the girl to catch up with him. When she did so she noticed that that odd air of authority was back with him again.

"I'd still like to see how you live," he said, as she hesitated.

She delayed no more. She gave him one grim look—then she inserted her key in the lock of the second door along the corridor, opened it and switched on the lights. Thomas Smith paused and stood looking into the room.

"Untidy but cosy," Glenda explained. "Now I wish you would go. The regulations here don't permit men visitors. If you were seen here I'd be told to go and a place like this isn't easy to find these days. All these flats are tenanted by single girls."

"Really?" Thomas Smith brushed the issue aside and stepped into the room. His hat remained on; then as he caught a look from Glenda he seemed to sense what she was thinking for he took it off quickly and stood with it in his hand, gazing about him.

Glenda did not say anything. Just at this moment she was too interested in observing Thomas Smith in bight light for the first time. His features she had already seen in detail, but not his head. He had a very high brow, his black hair flattened back from it after the fashion of popular drawings of Mephisto. He gave the impression of having intelligence far beyond the average.

"I like it," he decided finally.

"Yes, it's quite comfortable," Glenda said, her voice cool.

He looked at the TV set. "And what is this?"

"Don't tell me you don't recognize a television set!"

He smiled. "It is so well disguised with all this ornamental work I hardly recognized it. The pictures are three-dimensional I assume?"

"What?" Glenda gave him a blank look.

Thomas Smith seemed inwardly amused. Glenda kept her ear cocked for the coming of the landlady, but nothing transpired. Then Thomas Smith said: "I don't in any way wish to embarrass you, and you are obviously worried as to what might happen if I should be found here."

"I'm glad you see it my way at last!"

"My wish to see your dwelling over-ruled my regard for your feelings, I'm afraid. Before I go, though, there is something I would like to ask: Would you mind being my guide whilst I become accustomed to London?"

"I—er—don't quite know what to say to that."

"Yes you do. You want to say 'Yes' but you feel unsure of me."

Glenda opened her mouth and then shut it again.

"You needn't be uncomfortable." Thomas Smith raised his dark eyes suddenly, fixing them on Glenda with a mystifying, penetrating power. "I shall never willingly cause you a moment's embarrassment, and I feel you are the kind of woman to familiarize me with the city. In whatever time you can spare, of course."

"Today is Friday," Glenda mused. "I am not likely to be sent on another meteorite assignment, or anything so crazy as that, so perhaps—"

"Meteorite assignment? When?"

"Today. I had to cover the story of some fallen chunks of iron in Sussex. The Meteorites fell last night and lit up the whole countryside. All I found was hot iron, some of it with rivets in it. That's already given sundry scientists a headache. Rivets in a meteorite! That's definitely something new!"

"Yes, indeed it is." Thomas Smith looked thoughtful for a moment and then he smiled. "Then you may have some free time?"

"I'll have some on Sunday. Since it is too big a risk for you to come here we'd better meet somewhere. Say Marble Arch at two-thirty?"

"I'll try and find it," he promised, moving to the door. "And thank you so much, Miss Carlyle."

"Oh—one moment!" Glenda exclaimed. "If something should turn up and stop my meeting you, where can I get in touch with you in time to let you know?"

"I don't quite know—yet. I have no fixed address. However, if you should be prevented from meeting me I can always get in touch with you afterwards, either here or at the *Clarion* offices."

"Yes, of course."

"Goodnight, Miss Carlyle." Thomas Smith smiled gravely seemed to have notions about shaking hands, and went silently away down the stairs.

Outside he walked aimlessly, and was soon in the slums of Somers Town, part of the old-word London with its twisted streets and numberless diagonal and cross-crossing alleys. Suddenly he stopped and looked up sharply. To his right was a low building that might have belonged to the Dickensian era.

It was not the desperate scream of a woman that stopped the stranger. The scream came some seconds after he had paused and sensed something. Before the scream came he had already singled out the building from which it emanated and, with an agile leap, he caught at a ledge and hauled himself up quickly. In a matter of moments he had reached the window on the second floor, smashed his elbow through the glass, and tumbled into the room beyond.

It was gloomy but not entirely dark. There was the sound of harsh breathing from two different parts of the room. Then a man's voice blasted forth—coarse and choked with fury:

"What the devil do you want in here?"

Thomas Smith remained motionless. There was the sudden flaring of a match and a candle glowed. Amber light showed a woman fully dressed lying half across a bed, stark terror in her expression. The man, nearer the light, was standing in shirt and trousers, a large pair of scissors in a massive hand.

"Get outa here!" he grated.

Thomas Smith remained expressionless. "You would not expect me to leave here when you are about to murder your wife, would you?"

"I'm not murdering anybody, so—"

"Don't lie to me! You decided five minutes ago to murder your wife—apparently with those scissors. I don't intend to allow you to."

The woman rose into a half-sitting position as she spoke breathlessly. "I don't know how you got here, mister, but you're right. He was just about to run those scissors into me when you smashed the window—"

"Shut up!" the man snarled at her. "I'll deal with you later!"

"You will not deal with anybody, my friend," Thomas Smith stated quietly. "Get out of here, and don't ever come back!"

"You think I'll—"

The man stopped. The woman on the bed could not see Thomas Smith's face since he had turned his back on her, but she did see the expression which came to her husband's features. Blank, nameless fear rooted itself in his eyes as he stared fixedly. The scissors fell out of his hand—then in a sudden dive he headed for the window and scrambled through it. The stranger stood watching him until he had vanished from sight; then he turned to look at the woman on the bed and smiled at her.

"He'll kill me for sure now," she said. "The moment you're gone he'll come back and—"

"He'll never come back," Thomas Smith assured her gently. "Before an hour has passed he will be dead."

"You mean you're going to follow him up and kill him?"

"No. He will destroy himself. You may be confident of that. Henry will not interfere with your life any more."

"You knew him then? You must, to know his name."

"Let us say, madam, that I know what he planned to do, and leave it at that. From here on you may lead your life as you wish without Henry to upset you. Now, I must go."

The woman got off the bed and caught at the stranger's arm as he moved to the window. "Just a minute, mister. You knew what my husband planned to do, you say? What do you know about him? What's your name?"

"Thomas Smith."

"I never heard Henry mention that name."

"He hardly would. Goodnight, madam."

Then the stranger climbed through the narrow window again and dropped to the street. He paused when he reached the end of it. A dark figure lay in his path, motionless.

Stooping, he turned the figure over. It was dressed in only shirt and trousers and the mouth gaped. The eyes stared blankly into the night.

Thomas Smith left the body where it was and continued on his way.

CHAPTER TWO

Confession of murder

It was nearly an hour later when Thomas Smith came to a park and sat down on a bench seat. For quite a time he was motionless, looking into the sky. Then a policeman approached him and said, "Afraid I'll have to ask you to move on, sir."

"Why?"

"Sorry, sir, but you know the regulations as well as I do. No sleeping in the park."

"I'm not sleeping: only thinking. In fact I don't remember when last I did sleep. Must be a very long time ago."

"I'm afraid you'll have to move on."

"Why is the park left open if one is not supposed to come into it?"

"It isn't practical to shut it off. I patrol here every night, moving on tramps—and others."

"Then you have two separate laws? One for the day and the other for the night? It wouldn't matter if I slept here during the daytime?"

"No, sir." The Constable cleared his throat. "I don't make the laws. I just see they are carried out."

"Since you have a job to do, I'll move on." Thomas smith stood up. "That is, unless you'd care to stay and talk to me for a while."

"I'm not supposed to, sir. I've a patrol to make and a given time at which to report to headquarters."

"I see. In other words you do certain things because other people order you to, and they in turn take their instructions from somebody higher up still?"

"Yes, sir." The constable reflected. "I never quite saw it like that before. I suppose all of us take orders. We don't sort of question it: we just do it. Otherwise there'd be chaos."

"Are you quite sure there isn't already?" Thomas Smith asked. "My friend, the whole basic order of life nowadays is crazy—but how to readjust it I don't know."

"I'd suggest you don't try, sir," the constable said, satisfied by now that he was dealing with a crank.

"Nevertheless," the stranger mused, "it is an interesting problem. I must think about it. Goodnight, officer."

*   *   *

The following morning the Metropolitan police received two reports of death—apparently from natural causes. One concerned a tramp found dead in an alley off Fleet Street; and the other a man identified as Henry Armstrong, had been found dead in Somers Town. At first medical evidence suggested a form of apoplexy in each case; then later the reports were amended to mental derangement with heart failure.

One man was definitely interested, and that was the news editor of the *Clarion*. Promptly he called Glenda.

"There may be a story behind this," he told her. "Sudden and baffling death."

"Nothing baffling about it, chief. The two men died from mental derangement and heart failure, so—"

"Yes, but what deranged 'em? And why two of them? Just think how extraordinary a coincidence that is! You may not get far with the tramp in the Fleet Street alley since he had no identification upon him, but on the other chap you—" The news editor stopped and stared. "What's the matter with you, Glenny? Gone to sleep?"

Glenda had been staring into distance, her lips slightly parted. Now she gave a start.

"Did you say a tramp in a Fleet Street alley?"

"Uh-huh. I thought you knew."

"I didn't know where. It may make a difference."

The news editor frowned. "What's bitten you? Have you some inside line on this tramp?"

89

"Maybe. I can't work it out right now but I'll try and get the information you want."

"Out of him you'll get nothing. No identity, no anything. Just a drifting nobody. Try and get a line on the other fellow, Henry Armstrong. He was a gambler, as far as I can make out, making his living by his wits. His wife survives him, at 8 Chandos Street. She might have something to tell you."

Glenda took a taxi to the Armstrong abode. It was opened by a dark-headed, slovenly woman.

"Mrs. Armstrong?" Glenda asked.

"Yes, and if you're selling something—"

"Not a bit of it. I'm Glenda Carlyle of the *Clarion*. It concerns your husband's—er —unfortunate death. We have the official reports, but my editor thinks there may be a story behind them."

"Yes there is a story!" the woman agreed, quite excitedly. "I've been wondering what to do about it. I want somebody to tell it to."

"Good!" Glenda smiled and stepped inside. She took the chair the woman offered her and sat down.

"You see," Mrs. Armstrong said, "I have the queerest feeling that my husband was murdered. He was a rotten beast—but murder is still murder."

"Did you tell this to the police?"

"I haven't told anybody yet. It's only a suspicion after all, and because of my husband's death—or murder—saving me from being murdered myself I'm not pinning a charge on anybody."

"Just what happened?" Glenda asked.

"For you to print in your paper and perhaps get the man who saved me from death thrown into prison for life? No; that would be a shabby trick to play on him."

Glenda reflected. "The man you're referring to was tall, wasn't he, in a black hat and overcoat? Pale-faced, dark-eyed, and high cheekbones? I'll lay a bet that he just looked at your husband and never touched him."

"How did you know that?" the woman demanded, staring,

"Never mind. Did he give you his name?"

"Yes, but—"

"Was it Thomas Smith?"

The woman stared uneasily at Glenda. "I—I don't like this, Miss Carlyle! You must be a friend of his. When I think of the mysterious way he came here and saved me I don't know what to make of it."

"At the moment, Mrs. Armstrong, neither do I, but I do know Thomas Smith because he saved me last night from being assaulted by a tramp, just as he seems to have saved you from being murdered. We have that much in common. The coincidence of the two deaths satisfies me that Thomas Smith must have been responsible for both of them. Now how about telling me your side of it?"

The woman sat down slowly and related the incident of the night before in detail. Glenda sat listening intently.

"I just don't know what the man did," the woman finished, shrugging. "It seemed to me that he just looked at Henry and then Henry got out of the room by the window as fast as he could go. After that Mister Smith told me that my husband would be dead in a few hours. That is why I believe it must have been murder. But what sort of murder I don't know."

"The same thing happened with that tramp," Glenda said. "Mister Smith just looked at him and the tramp fled—screaming. I didn't know he would die. Mister Smith did not refer to that possibility, but he was found dead this morning."

"When the police came to see me about my husband, and had me identify him, I simply said that he'd dashed out into the night. I didn't say anything more, but I've been wondering since what really did happen. You've had some experience with crime, Miss Carlyle, so what do you think?"

Glenda shook her head. "I don't know. I've never heard of anybody being killed in such a queer way before." She roused herself and got to her feet. "Anyhow, Mrs. Armstrong, I shan't report what you have told me. I'll work out some kind of story to satisfy my editor without hinting at murder. Perhaps I'm wrong. If so I'll risk it, That tramp, and apparently your husband too, deserved all they got and I don't like putting Mister Smith in a spot because of it."

"Neither do I. He freed me from years of misery and fear with Henry, and far from thinking of him as a murderer I consider him a benefactor. It may not be a nice thing to say but it's the truth."

Glenda made no further comment. She shook hands and departed. On the way back to the *Clarion* offices she detoured into a small park and sat thinking things out for a while; then she wrote up a report that contained nothing indicative of the enigmatic Thomas Smith. The moment she returned to the office she typed the report out and took it in to the news editor.

He read it and then aimed a questioning glance. "Best you can do, Glenny?"

"'Fraid so."

"Listen, I know you inside out, and I think you're keeping something back."

"Why on earth should I?"

"I dunno. When you left here this morning you said you had some lead on the business—yet now you hand me this yarn about a woman beleaguered by her brutal husband, and said husband throwing some kind of mental storm and then vanishing into the night. It won't do, Glenny."

"I'm sorry, chief, but it's all I can turn in. Why all this fuss over a broken-down gambler and a good-for-nothing tramp? They're not headline news, anyway."

"They might become so before long," the news editor snapped. "Take a look at this: it's the latest opinion of Scotland Yard's best psychiatric and medical division."

Glenda took the report handed to her and studied it. She hardly needed to read it for the news editor's voice began to repeat it in its essence.

"They believe at the Yard that those two men were murdered. First they said natural causes and now they've discovered that both men had the conscious areas of their brains destroyed as though by electricity or something, causing rapid death. That spells murder, of the most fantastic, unheard-of kind of thing."

"It sounds to me as though these experts can't make up their minds," Glenda answered at length, putting the report back on the desk.

"You know better than that, Glenny. Our job is to get a lead if we can, and I believe you've got one. What about it?"

"The only line I had, was to try Henry Armstrong's wife—and that I did. There's my report on what she said."

"And she didn't say anything more?"

Glenda was silent. The news editor kept his eyes on her.

"Glenny, I'm asking for whatever gen you have, because if you don't hand it out somebody else will. I'll have to send Edwards if all else fails, and if he starts trying to make Mrs. Armstrong give a different story—"

"Not Edwards!" Glenda protested. "Please, chief! Give me a bit more time on this job. Make it my exclusive assignment to sort it out, then maybe I'll get a really good story for you. I'm just not sure of all my facts at the moment."

"All right," the news editor shrugged. "Sort it out as best you can. The police are looking into the business."

"You mean they're really working on the assumption of murder?"

"Exactly. Murder of a new type and therefore sensationally interesting."

Glenda sighed. "All this hullabaloo over a broken-down gambler and a lecherous tramp. Both are better off the face of the earth."

The news editor's eyes sharpened. "Who said anything about a lecherous tramp?"

"I did. I know he was, because he attacked me last night. I'm sure it's the same man. It was the same alley."

"Girl of my life, it's a story! A personal write-up from your angle, and—"

"I'm not writing anything up— yet!" Glenda nearly shouted. "You must give me time to clear this up. Otherwise it may involve somebody whom I know—and respect."

"For instance?"

"A man friend of mine, but he isn't a killer. It's just that he might seem to be mixed up in it, and I'm certainly not going to give him away. Let me prove first that he had nothing to do with it, and then I'll give you a story which you can slap all over the front page."

"Well, all right: but get the story fast. It's too hot to hold."

"I'm hoping to nail it down tomorrow—Sunday."

"I can't wait that long. The whole thing may be ancient history by then if the police move extra fast."

"Well, I—" Glenda stopped and swung around as the office boy came in. The news editor glared at him.

"Well, what do you want?"

"There's a man waiting to see Miss Carlyle," the lad explained. "Says it's pretty important."

Glenda moved. "Probably something to do with the women's page," she said quickly. "I did ask a man to look in this morning. We'll finish this little matter later, chief—"

"We'll finish it now!" he cut in, and banged the desk "This man can wait, whoever he is. Hop it, Terry. Tell the man to wait—"

The news editor paused. The door had opened quietly and Thomas Smith stood there, gazing into the office with that curious air of mild surprise that always seemed to pervade him. When his eyes settled on

Glenda he removed his hat and came forward. The news editor sat in silence, summing up the visitor, looking at his high forehead, his quiet attire, his polished black hair.

"I gather, sir, that you don't stand on ceremony?" he asked, and Thomas Smith turned to him.

"Forgive my coming in like this, but I wanted to have a word with Miss Carlyle. Quickly."

The news editor jerked his head and the office boy hurried out. Glenda hesitated and then said: "This is Mister Smith, chief. A—a friend of mine."

"A friend, or the friend?"

"The friend," Thomas Smith answered then in the same easy tone he added: "I think it is high time that Miss Carlyle was spared the task of trying to defend me for apparent murder. I appreciate it, of course, but it is quite unnecessary."

The news editor said: "What do you want with Miss Carlyle? Or am I not supposed to ask?"

"I just wanted to enquire from her why the authorities should think it murder to destroy two men who were too foul to live. I notice in the newspapers that murder is suspected, and that is apparently contrary to law."

"Are you trying to be funny?" the news editor snapped. "Since when has murder been anything else but a crime?"

"I suppose," Thomas Smith mused, "it would not be called murder to isolate and destroy a dangerous germ? To exterminate a human pest is no greater crime than to obliterate a disease, both being inimical to life."

"In heavens' name, what is all this about?" the news editor demanded. "What are you getting at?"

Thomas Smith shrugged. "I realize that the authorities are looking for the cause of the death of two men last night, and so I am here to explain matters. As I said earlier, it occurred to me that Miss Carlyle might be trying to shield me."

"Mister Smith, don't you realize what you're doing? Glenda exclaimed in alarm. "You're condemning yourself to a life sentence in prison! If this were the United States, you'd be facing the death penalty!"

"Am I? Why?"

"Why? Because murder is the ultimate crime! If you go on talking like this it'll be a confession of guilt and nothing will be able to save you."

Thomas Smith reflected and then drew up a chair. He set it for Glenda to seat herself and then he took another chair at an angle between the girl and the news editor. The news editor drew his notepad towards him.

"I am a law unto myself," Thomas Smith said. "When I decide a certain move shall be made, I make it, without consideration for anything or anybody. For that reason I decided that both that tramp and Henry Armstrong needed eliminating. So they were eliminated. There is nothing more to it than that."

"You will soon find yourself answering to the police, Mister Smith."

Thomas Smith gave his odd smile. "Evidently I did not make it quite clear that I acknowledge no law."

"Nobody can escape it, especially when you make a frank confession like this before witnesses."

The news editor sat back and lighted his pipe slowly.

"Why do you do that?" the stranger asked.

"Do what?"

"Inhale smoke and then exhale it. I assume it has some kind of purpose? I have observed quite a few people doing it,"

"What the devil are you talking about, man? Don't tell me you've never seen anybody smoke before!"

"Mister Smith has been away from civilization," Glenda put in quickly. "Amazonian forests, didn't you say, Mister Smith?"

"Certainly a long way from here," he replied ambiguously. "Getting back to the subject, I have been wondering what precise benefit is extracted from this smoking ritual."

"Benefit, none; pleasure, plenty," the news editor grunted. "All right, so you're a crank with queer ideas on people's habits. What about your habit of killing people whom you don't think fit to live? I want the facts!"

"I have given them. I wiped out those two men. What more do you want me to say?"

"I want the interesting little bit which goes in between and which should explain how you did it."

"Oh!" Thomas Smith smiled. "I don't propose to explain that, and I doubt very much if anybody will ever be able to solve the matter."

"It's partly solved already," Glenda put in. "The experts think that an electrical machine, or something like it, destroyed the conscious area of the brain in each man."

"Ingenious, but incorrect," Thomas Smith commented. "Besides, in the case of the tramp you saw for yourself that I had no—machine, or similar contrivance. I simply ordered the tramp away, and he went. Later he died."

"If you won't explain it the police can find the solution for themselves," the news editor remarked. "Right now I'm going to print your confession all over the front page, and in duty bound I cannot allow you to leave here without a police officer interviewing you."

"So says the law?" Thomas Smith asked dryly.

"I'm afraid so." The news editor looked at Glenda. "Sorry, Glenny, but I've got to do it."

She nodded morosely and watched him reach for the telephone. Then he paused. He sat back in his chair, took his pipe from between his teeth, and pondered.

"Something the matter?" Thomas Smith enquired.

"I—I just can't think what I was going to telephone about! Of all the queer things! Went clean out of my head—just like that!" For a moment the news editor scowled and drummed his fingers on the desk; then he sighed. "No use. Just lost it. You know how it is."

"But you—" Glenda started speaking and then stopped.

"What?"

"Nothing. Nothing at all." Glenda's eyes switched to Thomas Smith as he sat smiling.

"No use, just can't think of it," news editor sighed. "Anyway, sir, perhaps you will tell me your name, and why you are here?"

Glenda's jaw sagged for a moment. In complete incredulity she looked at her chief.

"My name is Thomas Smith," the stranger said. "I have a few interesting details which might suit Miss Carlyle for the women's section. All I need is your permission for her to accompany me to—a place of importance."

"Up to her," the news editor responded. "She's her own boss when it comes to the women's section."

Thomas Smith nodded and got to his feet. The news editor rubbed his chin once or twice, then he turned back to his job and took no further notice as Glenda hurried out ahead of the stranger. The moment the news editor's door was shut Glenda came to a halt.

"Mister Smith, how did you—"

"Not here," he murmured, with a glance about the busy office. "Let us go somewhere where we can talk."

Glenda nodded and whipped her hat and coat from the stand. In a few minutes she and Thomas Smith were out in Fleet Street. As they walked along he had that queer smile on his lean, pale features.

"I've got to have an explanation!" Glenda insisted. "There is something uncanny about you. Somehow you stopped my editor dead in his tracks—so completely that he seems to have forgotten all about the murder of those two men."

"He has—completely," Thomas Smith agreed. "Nor will he remember what he intended doing about it."

"But he'll remember when he comes to his reports on the matter!"

"No he won't. Doubtless he will print all the information he has to date, but he will not recall anything about my connection with it. All he will recollect about me is that I called to offer you a story for the women's page."

Glenda gave a glance of hopeless bewilderment. It widened the smile on Thomas Smith's face. "Why so troubled, Miss Carlyle? You tried in the first instance to protect me, didn't you? Further, you hesitated when you had the chance to remind the news editor of his plan to call the police."

"What makes you so sure that I tried to protect you?"

"I know you did. Let's leave it at that."

"I wish I could—but you don't seem to realize how impossible this whole business is! What is this peculiar power you seem to have? This ability to slay people as you like, to make others forget, to know in advance what folks intend doing?"

"Does it frighten you?" he asked gently.

"A little—and yet, with you, I'm not afraid. It's hard for me to explain. One thing I always shall remember and it is that you saved me last night."

There was silence for a while as they both walked onwards. Presently Glenda nodded to a little side-street restaurant she often visited and within a few moments she and Thomas Smith were seated at a corner table in the quiet interior.

"Coffee and rolls," Glenda told the proprietor, and gave Thomas Smith an inquiring glance as he removed his hat.

"I'll try them," he said.

"Try them?" the proprietor repeated. "Nothing very original in coffee and rolls, is there?" and with a puzzled glance back over his shoulder he returned to the counter.

"Don't tell me that even coffee and rolls are new in your experience!" Glenda exclaimed helplessly.

"I'm afraid so. Having never tried either before I shall enjoy the experiment."

Glenda just sat and looked at him, her violet eyes wide. He smiled back at her.

"Getting back to cases," she said, when the coffee and rolls had been brought, "why did you really come to the office this morning?"

"I read of the murders and the construction being placed upon them. I knew you'd tie them up with me, so I thought I'd better take a hand before you got involved in difficult explanations. Thank you, Miss Carlyle, for protecting me so loyally. If you find yourself again facing the issue of my being a possible murderer, don't withhold anything. Simply send the person concerned to me and I'll deal with him—or her."

"But you'll get yourself life imprisonment for it! I've said that before! You don't seem to understand—"

"I understand everything, but I'm well able to take care of myself. I know that at the moment your one wish is that I'd explain everything, but that isn't so easy as it sounds. You have my promise though that I'll make things clear as soon as I can."

Glenda sighed. "Well, of course, I can't make you explain—but I'm losing the greatest story in years and doing nothing about it."

Thomas Smith tasted his coffee, reflected, and then tasted it again. Presently he asked a question.

"I mean no more to you than just a story? Is that it?"

"I'm a newspaper woman, Mister Smith. I've been trained to forget everything else but that. To me, you are a man of fascinating possibilities, and yet I cannot translate any of those possibilities into writing. I find it pretty hard to bear. All I know of you is that you are courteous, can stamp people out by simply looking at them, can make a hard-boiled editor forget, and can tell with uncanny accuracy what I am thinking about. Do you think any news writer was ever so loaded with highspots and couldn't use them?"

"You will—one day. In the meantime I'm glad you are going to be my guide as you promised. You said tomorrow, but there's no reason why it can't be today, is there? Your editor gave you permission to come out with me."

"You said that if I got involved in having to explain your actions I could send the person concerned to you. Where do you live? Have you an address yet?"

"No, but I've been looking around. I rather fancy the *Zenith* Hotel."

"So do plenty of people," Glenda said dryly. "It'll cost you a fortune. It's one of the most exclusive hotels in the city."

"I see." Thomas Smith mused. "At the moment I have no money, a state of affairs I shall have to rectify."

"No money!" Glenda repeated blankly. "Then how did you get from South America, or wherever you were?"

"Oh, I managed . . . Apparently, though, money as such is not essential providing one has something of value that can be turned into cash. Is that correct?"

"Quite correct—but you'll need something mighty good to bring any money worthy of the prices charged in a hotel like the *Zenith!*"

"Gold, oil, diamonds and uranium seem to be the most valuable assets in existence," Thomas Smith said. "I have made a study of the matter."

The manner in which he referred to everything as though he had just discovered it again clouded Glenda's mind—then she forgot everything and the world seemed to turn inside out for a moment, as there appeared on the tablecloth from Thomas Smith's hand two of the most superb diamonds she had ever seen.

"Great heavens!" she gasped, and immediately covered them with her handbag. Thomas Smith looked at her in surprise.

"Why do that?"

"Do have sense!" Glenda pleaded. "You can't expect to go on living if you flash diamonds of that size around! If they are real diamonds?" She hesitated, breathing hard.

"Of course they are. Pure carbon."

Thomas Smith withdrew them from under the handbag and then came to sit at Glenda's side of the table. When he opened his palm a blaze of blue and vermilion fire seemed to consume it. Glenda gazed at the gems as if hypnotized.

"Where on earth did you get them?" she asked at last. "Why, even the Koh-i-noor would look cheap beside these. They're as big as hens' eggs!"

"Yes, they are rather lovely," Thomas Smith agreed, closing his hand over them again. "As to where I obtained them—well, I just happened to know where to look."

"What you really mean is that you found a source of diamonds in some unexplored spot in Brazil. That it?"

"Brazil is certainly full of riches," he murmured.

Glenda sat back and mused, a look of dawning understanding struggling over her features. "Your South American activities, whatever they may have been—or was it the Amazon country?—explain one or two things to me. I'll make a guess—that you stumbled on some ancient civilization that had left many of its secrets behind. It gave you powers beyond the average, and the diamonds came from the same source. Am I right?"

"It is worth a speculation," he answered then he returned the diamonds to his pocket and asked a question. "I imagine some gem dealer would be glad to have these diamonds. Whom do you suggest?"

"Well, there's Chantry's, just off New Bond Street. They are a famous and reputable firm."

"Good. We'll go there next."

Glenda delayed no longer over the coffee and rolls. In a few moments, she having paid for the refreshment, they left the restaurant. In another half-an-hour they were in a private room of Chantry's with David Chantry himself, a delicate-looking middle-aged man with white hair, studying the gems through his lens. Then he weighed them.

"Remarkable," he commented at length, laying the diamonds on the velvet square on his desk after weighing them. "Positively remarkable. I've never seen such fluidity, such beauty, or such size! The original Koh-i-noor, which in its first state weighed seven-hundred-and-ninety-three carats, cannot compare with these precious stones, Mister Smith. One weighs eight-hundred-and-twelve carats, and the other eight-hundred-and-forty."

"Which, I gather, makes them of considerable value?" Thomas Smith enquired, smiling pleasantly.

The gem dealer gave him an odd glance. "Mister Smith, these diamonds can make you a millionaire several times over, and I am prepared to purchase them, but first I must have the details of their history. I must know all about them."

"Why?"

"It is customary procedure. One does not buy such gems without knowing at least the reason for their sale."

"I cannot see that the reason has anything to do with it," Thomas Smith responded. "You have here two diamonds which your experience assures you are genuine. I require money in exchange. Nothing could be simpler than that."

"Unfortunately it is not so simple as that. I wish I had not to touch on so delicate a subject, but I am afraid I must. These diamonds may be—hmm—stolen property."

"Ridiculous," Thomas Smith said calmly.

"Mister Smith, you must appreciate that gems of this size don't exist in the ordinary way. They are usually relics of a bygone dynasty, the property of a race now vanished from the earth. The gems of a king or queen perhaps. Every great gem has a history, and I want the history of these."

"I found them in South America, but the exact spot, and in what circumstances, I refuse to divulge. That would not be prudent."

Chantry sighed. "For the time being, then, I would suggest that you retain these gems—and in a very safe place—while I make the usual enquiries. Then we can talk business again. Formalities must be observed, I'm afraid."

Thomas Smith stood up, tall, expressionless. His long index finger pointed at the gems steadily as they blazed and glittered on the velvet square.

"I appreciate," he said, "that you have certain technicalities to consider, but I do not propose to be subjected to them. To me, this is a clear-cut case of a business deal, and you are receiving two perfectly genuine diamonds in return for an agreed figure. What is that figure?"

"Chantry hesitated, looking straight into Thomas Smith's dark eyes. For some reason the gem dealer could not move his gaze away. He fumbled awkwardly for words.

"At present market value," he said presently, "I am prepared to offer you two million pounds."

Thomas Smith moved his eyes to look at Glenda. "Do you think that is a fair figure, Miss Carlyle?"

"Fair!" She gulped slightly. "I would certainly think so, but I'm no expert."

"Three million is the figure I want," Thomas Smith decided, and turned back to Chantry again. "You said yourself that they would make me a millionaire several times over, Mister Chantry. Your check for that amount will be satisfactory."

"But I—"

"Now!" Thomas Smith finished, and since she was seated a little to the rear of him Glenda could not see his expression. In any case she was not concentrating on that: she was watching in fascination as, all thoughts of an investigation apparently gone to the winds, David Chantry drew a check book from the desk drawer, unscrewed a fountain-pen cap mechanically, and began to write. There was only the sound of the traveling nib and then the rasp of the paper as the check was torn from its counterfoil perforations.

"Thank you," Thomas Smith said quietly. "I can assure you Mister Chantry, that you will have no cause to regret your bargain." He glanced at Glenda. "If you are ready, Miss Carlyle?"

Glenda got to her feet and shot a look at the gem dealer. He was sitting looking fixedly at the gems as though they had chained him body and soul. He did not even look up as the two left his office. They passed through the main area of the, shop and so gained the outdoors again.

"Two gems, one slip of paper," Thomas Smith mused, looking at the check as he walked along. "It seems a queer exchange. I suppose I should put this in a bank?"

Glenda had a hard job to keep a hold on herself. "But of course! What else did you expect? That paper is convertible into a three million in hard cash any time you want it."

"And when I wish to draw a percentage of the sum, what do I do? Ask for it?"

"You write a check for the amount you want and you will be paid the equivalent of that amount as long as your credit holds good."

"You're a wonderful guide, Miss Carlyle," Thomas Smith said, smiling down upon her. "I'm most grateful."

"I don't mind helping you, but I would like some kind of reward—an explanation of your behavior, for instance. You did something to Mister Chantry, didn't you? Made him obey you? He'd never have given you his check so easily otherwise."

"I saw no point in an investigation. As I have mentioned before I acknowledge no law except my own. I gave him a square deal and he, I think, gave me one. There the matter ends as far as I am concerned."

"Do you mean that he will never know why he wrote that check without investigating first?"

"For twelve hours he will have difficulty in remembering me but after that he will recall the details and, possibly, start an investigation on which he has obviously set his heart. However, it will not signify then: this money will have been lodged in a bank for me to use. It is imperative to me that I get money immediately, and— Ah! Would this be a bank?"

Thomas Smith came to a halt and surveyed an edifice of glazed granite.

"Would this be—?" Glenda gave herself a little shake. "Yes, it's a bank. Do you want me to come in with you?"

"If you would. I'm not too sure of procedure."

"We wish to see the manager, please," Glenda found herself saying to a clerk behind the glassed counter; and before long the manager was completely poker-faced in his office whilst he impassively studied the check for three million pounds.

"If you will pardon me?" he said politely, and picked up the telephone: "Get me Mister Chantry, the gem dealer, please."

CHAPTER THREE
Miracle cure

There was a pause. Thomas Smith sat listening to the one-sided conversation that followed, Glenda moving her gaze from him to the bank manager. Then at last the manager returned the 'phone to its rest and smiled.

"Everything is in order, Mister Smith," he said cordially.

"Did you expect it to be otherwise?"

"Great heavens, no! Just a formality, you understand."

"I'm afraid I don't. There is so much formality and regulation impregnated into the normal business of living that it becomes difficult to live at all!"

"Quite, quite," the manager agreed, with a queer look. "However, I will attend to this matter immediately, Mister Smith. You—er—wish to make a withdrawal now?"

"I will consider it whilst you arrange the account. I wish to consult this young lady here."

"Ah, of course! Very good." The manager rose, took up the check, and left the office.

"Please don't consult me on how to handle a fortune!" Glenda protested. "I just wouldn't know what to do with it!"

"Are you afraid of money?" Thomas Smith asked.

"By no means, but the thought of that amount of money makes me dizzy."

"How extraordinary! There should be enough and to spare if a community is well organized, but of course it isn't: I have become increasingly aware of that fact. Too many laws, too many ridiculous regulations, uncertainty. However, how much do you think I might need for immediate expenses?"

Glenda reflected. "If you are staying at the *Zenith* you'll naturally pay by check. As to immediate needs . . . Well, say a thousand, and that's on the top side."

"We'll call it two thousand and be on the safe side," Thomas Smith decided, smiling, and two thousand it was. When he and Glenda left the bank he had the money, made up in various high denominations, together with a check book, in an inside pocket.

"I ought to be getting back to the office," Glenda said. "My boss will be wondering what has happened to me."

"He gave you permission to roam, Miss Carlyle, and that is what I suggest we do. I had thought of a lunch and an afternoon together in which I might get orientated to London."

"I'd love it, but if I abuse my freedom I might get the sack."

"The sack? What sack?"

"I mean fired. Discharged!"

"Oh? What a curious expression." Thomas Smith walked on for a while with Glenda beside him. Then he asked: "Would that matter? Suppose I gave you a couple of diamonds worth a few million or so?"

Glenda halted. Thomas Smith did so too, an odd twinkle in his dark eyes.

"Don't ever say such things," Glenda whispered. "Not even in fun."

"I assure you I'm quite serious. I can get as many diamonds as I wish, and as big as I wish. Any time you want any just ask mc. I shall not press you to accept since it seems to cause you embarrassment."

"Being offered diamonds worth millions is enough to embarrass anybody!" Glenda exclaimed as they resumed walking.

Thereafter conversation veered for a while to more commonplace topics. Thomas Smith asked a variety of questions as they strolled along—questions concerning buildings traffic, climate, and Glenda answered everything in tireless detail. All the time she kept asking herself how it had all come about, and why she had so willingly become the slave of this strange young man with the genteel manners.

It was half-past twelve when Thomas Smith seemed satisfied with the information he had obtained so he and Glenda retired to a restaurant for lunch.

"Don't you think," Glenda asked, when the meal was before them, "that it is time to come to some sort of understanding?"

He looked surprised. "In what way?"

"Well, to say the least of it, our friendship is the queerest one I ever heard of! You have mysterious powers and can produce diamonds of fabulous value as easily as pebbles—while I, on the other hand, keep answering questions which by all normal rules you should never need to ask. Doesn't that mean that we ought to know one another better? I want to know why you behave as you do, and in turn I'll tell you anything I possibly can."

"If there were anything I wanted to know about you personally, Miss Carlyle, I'd have asked you long ago," Thomas Smith replied. "As it is, I know you work on the *Clarion*, not because you are best fitted for it but because you have to work as you do because of your mother—widowed and a cripple."

"That's the sort of thing I mean!" Glenda exclaimed. "Without my explaining anything you know all about me."

"It saves time, doesn't it?"

"I suppose so, but it is disconcerting. I can never be sure whether or not you know my thoughts."

Thomas Smith smiled, reflected, then asked a question. "What exactly is the matter with your mother? In medical terms?"

"An extreme case of arthritis," Glenda answered moodily. "She is confined to a wheel-chair. There's nobody other than myself to support her since I have no brothers or sisters. Dad died ten years ago."

Thomas Smith gave his peculiar smile. "Quite a loyal, honest young woman, are you not?" He patted her hand gently. "Loyal to your mother and loyal to me, yet inwardly worried as to what might happen if you keep on being loyal to me . . . On my account you have nothing to fear. I can give you everything in the world you can want if you will but remain at my side."

"Some girls," Glenda said seriously, "might interpret that as a proposal of marriage."

"It was not meant in that sense. It never can be." Thomas Smith brushed the issue aside as though he were half afraid of it, the first sign of uncertainty he had ever revealed.

"Of course," Glenda smiled. "You are not the kind of man a girl can fall in love with. You're—you're so different, like an elder brother, a pleasant uncle from a distant country, or—something."

"I would like to meet your mother," Thomas Smith said.

"Nothing simpler. We could make it tomorrow."

"Why tomorrow when there is so much left of today?"

Glenda sighed. "You just will not realize that I have a job to do, will you? I've got to return to the office with my story—for which I am still waiting."

"If you return there by evening it will be soon enough and you will have your story as I promised . . . How does it happen that you don't live with your mother?"

"Because of the difficulty of getting to and from home. She lives in the same cottage where I was born about thirty miles out of London. A companion comes daily to help—so at least I feel that she is safe. The next-door neighbors have an eye to her, too."

"What do the doctors and surgeons say about her. Can she be cured?"

"She might by very expensive treatment—far more than I can afford. Arthritis is a difficult ailment to cure."

"On the contrary. It is no more difficult than any other trouble. It surprises me that the scientists and thinkers haven't worked much further towards eliminating diseases from the community. However, that is beside the point."

Glenda half started to say something and then thought better of it. She finished her meal in silence, nor did Thomas Smith comment further. This time he paid for the meal himself.

"The station is not far from here," Glenda said. "The train will get us there at—"

"I think it's time we had some quicker means of transport," Thomas Smith decided. "Across the street there I notice a showroom dealing in cars. Come along."

Glenda nodded rather dazedly, then she followed Thomas Smith into the enormous car-showroom. She looked in silent envy upon the gleaming creations around her.

"I assume these cars are driven by internal combustion engines?" Thomas Smith asked, as Glenda surveyed the models.

"Er—yes," She looked astonished. "Is there some other way?"

"I don't know. It surprises me that there is not considering the atomic bomb has been discovered—" Thomas Smith broke off as the immaculate salesman arrived and came level.

"Your pleasure, sir?" he enquired.

"Not my pleasure—the young lady's," Thomas Smith replied.

"What!" Glenda exclaimed. "You—you mean you want me to chose one?"

"For your own, yes. Though I cannot answer all the questions you wish to ask of me I can recompense you in some small way for your kindness in tolerating me. Choose which car you want."

"But—I can't! If you give me a car people will think things. It's as good as saying you—you mean something to me!"

"Well, don't I?"

"Yes, but not in that sense." Glenda stopped and shook her head firmly. "Sorry, I couldn't accept such a gift."

"But you want it, Miss Carlyle. If you have a comfortable conveyance you can take your mother out. It is not for you to listen to the biased opinions of others but to obey the dictates of your mind and heart—as I do. As long as you do no conscious wrong in pursuing your own particular desire you have nothing to fear. Now—choose a car."

"This is too absurd—yet too wonderful," Glenda murmured, looking about her. "The model I like best is that one. The . . . "

"Ah yes, madam. An exquisite car. Expensive of course but one cannot expect quality without paying for it."

"Petrol engine, of course?" Thomas Smith asked.

"Er—yes, sir. Yes indeed!" The salesman swallowed something.

"Science," Thomas Smith commented, "is a long way behind in powering engines with atomic force or solar energy. Maybe they will harness it in the next decade."

"Possibly so, sir."

Glenda was not listening to the conversation. Opening the door of the big car she slid into the seat and squirmed luxuriously as she fiddled with the gleaming controls.

"It's terrific!" she cried, as Thomas Smith looked in upon her "I've never seen anything so exquisite!"

"Do you think you'll have difficulty in driving it?" Thomas Smith asked.

"Not I! I've driven a car for years—a staff one which I can't use privately, I mean." Glenda's smile of rapture began to fade and she became solemn. "This is too magnificent for a workaday girl like me."

"The price?" Thomas Smith asked the salesman.

"Twenty five thousand pounds, sir."

Glenda jumped. Thomas Smith was looking at her. "The fact that you are a workaday girl has nothing to do with it, Miss Carlyle," he said.

"Yes I know, but—honestly, I—" Glenda's protest faded out. For one thing she was a woman at heart and it told her she would be an idiot to try and stop herself having a £25,000 car, and for another she knew that the inscrutable Thomas Smith would accept no refusal.

She was right. The details were rapidly completed and they then drove out to see her mother. When they had reached the cottage Thomas Smith followed the girl in and remained silent, hat in hand, as Glenda embraced the gray-haired woman in the wheel-chair. His gaze traveled about the quiet neatness of the room. It was low-ceilinged, filled with good but old-fashioned furniture. A log-effect electric fire glowed warmly in the fireplace recess.

"And this is Mister Smith," he heard Glenda saying as she turned to him. "This is my mother, Mister Smith."

"This is quite a pleasure," Glenda's mother said. "From what Glenda has been telling me, you are quite an extraordinary young man."

Glenda changed the subject abruptly. "What do you think of that car out there, mum?"

She drew back the net curtains so her mother could see as far as the gate.

"I saw it arrive, Glenny, and I just couldn't think who it could be—"

"It's mine! Mister Smith gave it to me in return for—for services rendered. I'll be able to take you out for rides now."

Mrs. Carlyle looked from the car to her daughter; then up to Thomas Smith's calm, pale face.

"Mister Smith, what does this mean?" she asked deliberately. Then, looking sharply at her daughter: "Glenny, does it mean that you and Mister Smith— No, I can't believe that," she broke off. "Not when you call him 'Mister Smith' instead of by his Christian name."

"It's all such a tangle," Glenda sighed. "I'll try to explain in detail, then perhaps you'll understand."

Mrs. Carlyle listened patiently whilst the story was unfolded to her. During the narration Thomas Smith settled on a chair near the window and gazed absently over the countryside.

"But surely, Mister Smith," Mrs. Carlyle exclaimed finally, when the explanation was over, "there is some explanation for your unique gifts?"

"Indeed there is, madam, but I am not at liberty to divulge it."

"But it's all so utterly fantastic!" Mrs. Carlyle declared. "Still, since

109

Glenny is a capable girl and well able to look after herself I do not propose to make any suggestions. Except that I would remark that she is right in saying that people will be bound to talk."

"Your daughter, Mrs. Carlyle, has decided to adopt my own method and ignore the valueless comments of others following only her own judgment. The surest way to crush gossip is to ignore it."

"If one can." Mrs. Carlyle's face was troubled "I find this matter so delicate, so difficult to understand. It is not as though Glenda had brought home to me a young man who wishes to marry her. She has brought home some—"

"Someone stranger than anybody you ever met?" Thomas Smith asked, and laughed.

Glenda said: "Mr. Smith has been so long away from civilized life that he's having to learn all over again and I'm helping him all I can."

Mrs. Carlyle became silent and Glenda took advantage of the interval to make some tea. Whilst she did it Thomas Smith reflected and then said: "Apart from wishing to have the pleasure of knowing you, Mrs. Carlyle, I also wish to help you."

"With money perhaps? Or diamonds?" Mrs. Carlyle shook her head. "I think not, young man, thank you all the same. For one thing I have little use for money, and for another it would be useless, in my condition, even if you gave me the world."

"I can give you what you want most—freedom."

Mrs. Carlyle looked at the stranger fixedly, her expression one of utter bewilderment. He remained looking at her steadily, then he got to his feet.

"I notice," he said, drawing back the window curtain, "that there are some flowers in the garden here, just poking their heads over the winter soil."

"Crocuses," Glenda said. "They come up this time every year."

"They would look pretty on the table in a vase," Thomas Smith commented, musing.

"But they'd quickly die," Glenda pointed out. "They are bulb plants, and once cut off from—"

"They will never die." Thomas Smith turned from the window. "I think you had better go and pick them, Mrs. Carlyle."

"I?" She looked at him with wide eyes. "But how utterly ridiculous!"

"Please go," Thomas Smith said, and turned to her.

Glenda saw his profile, and then his back as he moved to face Mrs.

Carlyle directly. She gazed at him then with deliberate movements she unwrapped the blanket from about her legs, put her feet on the floor, and stood up. Utterly stunned Glenda watched her leave the room and the chill wind of winter blew through the cottage.

There seemed to be an interminable interval then Mrs. Carlyle returned, wind-blown, smiling in a half-puzzled fashion, the flowers in her hand. Thomas Smith closed the door behind her and stood watching as she slipped the flowers into a glass vase and then held it under a running tap in the back kitchen. Returning into the room she set the vase of flowers on the table.

"Mister Smith, what have you done?" Glenda cried suddenly, leaping up and seizing his arm. "Mother is walking! Walking! She hasn't done that since she was taken ill—"

"What are your own reactions, Mrs. Carlyle?" Thomas Smith asked.

She was smiling: "I feel a sense of extreme comfort, of optimism, of happiness—something I have never known since childhood. As though at one sweep all care has been lifted from me . . . What you have done I do not know. It is so utterly miraculous I can't even talk about it."

"You mean this cure isn't just some hypnotic performance?" Glenda demanded. "It won't wear off in an hour or two and put mother right back where she started?"

Thomas Smith laughed outright—the most human laugh Glenda had ever heard him give.

"Of course not! That wheel-chair can be used for firewood for all the need you'll have of it."

"That's right," Mrs. Carlyle agreed, as she met her daughter's astonished eyes. "What has happened I don't know, but I do know I'm cured . . . I believe," she added, thinking, "that it is not for me to question such things. Accept it for what it is, and be eternally grateful. As I am, Mr. Smith. Who you are, what you are, I do not know—but certainly my daughter could not be in better hands."

"That is how I have always felt," Glenda said. "It is the reason why I stay beside him in spite of everything. Nothing else seems to have any significance. He dominates without being dominating. He knows so much, yet seems so puzzled by everybody and everything . . . he has to have a guide. You see that, mother, don't you?"

She nodded, still smiling.

Thomas Smith turned to look at the flowers. They were glowing in full brilliant color as a momentary shaft of pale winter sunlight fell upon them through a window.

"Those will never die," he said somberly. "You'll see."

* * *

Glenda left her car in a garage near her mother's home and returned to town with Thomas Smith by train. She spoke but little on the way, her emotions too completely overwhelmed by the miracle of her mother's recovery. Now and again she found the stranger smiling at her inscrutably, that queer light of profound wisdom kindling in his dark eyes.

It was early evening when they reached London and both of them were aware as they left the station of the news placards of the evening papers. Glenda slowed to a halt as she caught sight of a nearby newsstand:

MENTAL MURDERS— NEW POLICE MOVES

"How do you suppose this has happened?" she asked.

Thomas Smith mused, then he bought a copy of the *Clarion*, and with Glenda beside him read the disquieting columns about himself.

"From the look of things," she said at length, giving him an anxious glance, "my editor has remembered something about you in spite of what you did to him. The police apparently know that it was you who wiped out that tramp and Henry Armstrong—and only my editor could have told them."

"I don't think so," Thomas Smith said. "Your editor could not have remembered that confession I made in his office. The only other answer is that the police must be smarter than I imagined. In any case, it's nothing to worry about."

"But it is!" Glenda insisted. "The police will be after you. You've got to hide—get away quickly."

"No, Miss Carlyle, I am going to carry straight on with my original intention and domicile myself at the *Zenith* hotel. If the police want me they know where to find me—and you may rest assured I'll be fully able to cope with the situation."

When Glenda reached the *Clarion* building, she went straight to her editor's office.

"Get the story?" he asked.

"Yes—a new slant on women of today by a man who's been away from civilization for several years."

The news editor took the copy and said: "This doesn't look like it's been typed on your usual machine. What happened?"

"I've been back home where I could concentrate. I used my own. My travels took me that far, so I thought I might as well work in comfort."

"Mmmm. Well, you've certainly got an angle here." The news editor's brows rose as he read the copy. "Who gave you the slant? That Thomas Smith individual who came here for you?"

"Yes. He's the one who's been away from civilization for such a long time."

"This stuff's good—very good," the news editor mused, still reading. "It compensates for the time you've been absent. Better writing than you have ever done before. But about this man Thomas Smith. There's far more to him than just his opinion of women after a long absence. He's heading for being the high spot in the weirdest murder trial of all time before long, and I shall want you to cover the story. You seem to be pretty well acquainted with him."

"You can't talk to a man like him without being," Glenda answered, sitting down.

"You've seen the headlines?"

Glenda nodded but did not say anything.

"The police are looking for that gent," the news editor explained. "It seems that the psychiatric and scientific experts at the yard are convinced that the tramp and Henry Armstrong, who were murdered last night, were killed by some dynamic mental force—and they know who did it."

"How can they know?" Glenda asked. "Unless you told them?"

"Unless I told them? Who do you think I am—Sherlock Holmes?"

Glenda was silent. It seemed, then, that Thomas Smith had spoken the truth when he had said that the news editor would not remember. There must be some other answer.

"I don't know a thing about the chap except that he wanted you so he could provide a story," the news editor mused. "I wish I'd known the facts about him at the time. I might have built up a better story. However, it seems that the police have for the second time interviewed the widow of Henry Armstrong and from her got particulars of man who fits this Thomas Smith individual in every particular."

"So that's it." Glenda muttered. "She gave him away."

"So what? What are you talking about? It's a public service to name a murderer, isn't it?"

"Not when he's also a benefactor with miraculous powers."

"Look—" The news editor strained forward. "Are you and I talking the same language, Glenny?"

"I know another side to Thomas Smith, chief—a marvelous side, but I'm not permitted to write about it."

"Because he forbids it?" The news editor laughed cynically. "A killer isn't entitled to forbid anything. If you have facts about him, then write 'em. That's what you're paid for."

"I can't do it. He means too much to me."

"He what? Good God, don't tell me you're in love with that pale-faced mystery sadist!"

"No, it isn't love—" Glenda looked before her with distance in her eyes. "I can't explain it properly. I never felt about any other person as I do about him—and it still isn't love. It's a sort of respect—a tremendous admiration, a feeling that he knows so much and yet cannot do without me to help him."

"Hero-worship! He's got you moonstruck—you, the very last girl of whom I would have expected it. Anyway, I'm not standing for it." The news editor sniffed contemptuously. "I want all the gen you can get on him, complete with photographs. Take a camera, see him again, and get busy."

"You mean now?"

"Yes, now! By tomorrow he'll be under arrest and I want his picture and life story. Hop to it."

Without another word Glenda left the office. She had been on the very point of firing herself out of her job but an inner sense had cautioned her to refrain. While she went for a Press camera, two square-shouldered men watched the door of Room 49 open on the first floor of the *Zenith* Hotel. Thomas Smith, his black hair shining, his figure immaculate in a gray suit, looked out.

"Thomas Smith?" one of the men asked.

"Yes, I am he."

"I'm a police officer," the man said, displaying his warrant card. "Chief-Inspector Brough. This is Detective-Sergeant Cavendish. I'd like a word with you, sir."

Thomas Smith smiled. "By all means, gentlemen. Please come in and be seated."

The two men glanced at each other and then entered the room. The only illumination came from a tall, amber-shaded reading lamp. Thomas Smith closed the door and motioned to chairs.

The Chief-Inspector put his hat on the floor beside him and then said: "It is the matter of one Henry Armstrong—and an unidentified tramp—which concerns me, sir. They—"

"Have been found dead, presumed murdered by some mental process which your experts cannot explain, and you think I am responsible? Yes, gentlemen, I have read the papers."

"We obtained our information from—"

"Mrs. Armstrong. Yes, I know that too."

"How do you know?" Brough demanded, startled. "That statement was suppressed from publication. Only a few news editors know of it and they have not published the source of our information."

Thomas Smith smiled. "I know quite a lot, gentlemen, and—like the editors—I shall not divulge my source of information. Please proceed."

Brough cleared his throat and scowled somewhat. "Following our interview with Mrs. Armstrong—the second one we had with her—we traced your movements. We have no doubt whatever that you caused the deaths of Henry Armstrong and the tramp by some mental process best known to yourself. The process is puzzling, but we are not concerned with that, merely with the fact that murder has been done. For that reason I am charging you with the murder of Henry Armstrong, and of a man as yet unidentified, and I have to warn you that any statement you may make will be taken down in writing and may be used in evidence—"

Thomas Smith laughed good-humoredly. The Chief-Inspector scowled all the more and got to his feet.

"I must ask you to accompany me to—"

"To Scotland Yard, I suppose? Quite so, Inspector. However, I do not intend to accompany you to Scotland Yard or anywhere else. I freely admit I killed those two men you have mentioned, but only because they deserved it. Both of them treated women in a manner which made them unfit to live."

"That is beside the point, sir. There are further charges to be made. You recently came into possession of diamonds of fabulous value by obscure means."

"You surely don't call that a crime?"

"The law demands that precious stones must have their source of origin declared. I understand you refused to give that information when asked for it by Mister Chantry, the gem expert."

"So you have seen him also?"

"I have already said we traced your movements!" Brough barked. "If you have any statement to make concerning those diamonds—"

"Indeed I have!" Thomas Smith rose from his chair. "It is that you are exceeding your authority! Mister Chantry got his gems and I got his check. The law has no power to do anything about that."

"It has when you resorted to some kind of hypnosis to make Mister Chantry pay."

"So he has recovered, has he? Had he received paste diamonds in return for his money your accusation would have been justified: but the diamonds are genuine—as no doubt Mr. Chantry has admitted."

"Yes, but—"

"You have no case here, Inspector."

CHAPTER FOUR
Invisible man

Brough massaged his chin dubiously. "Maybe not as far as the stones themselves are concerned, but the hypnosis part definitely demands action. Even if there were not the far graver charge of murder I would still have to arrest you for practicing hypnosis to the danger of the public. That kind of thing, unless it is performed in a licensed theater, is not permitted."

"Inspector," Thomas Smith sighed, "I am commencing to wonder what is permitted —how anybody is able to do anything at all! One cannot move hand or foot without infringing some law or other."

"I hope, sir," Brough muttered, "you won't give trouble when I ask you to come along with us—now."

The stranger reflected. "Before we go, Inspector, may I ask where is your connecting link proving that because I visited Mrs. Armstrong's room in the dead of night I must of necessity be the murderer of Henry Armstrong and the tramp?"

"Connecting link?"

"Proof, then. You have no proof that I committed murder."

"You have admitted that you did so!" Brough retorted.

"That does not prove anything. When murder is committed one very often finds several people confessing to it—sometimes for vainglorious publicity reasons. I might deny all knowledge of the affair later on, and in that case you would need your own proof that I am the man you want. Where is it?"

"Just the same I have a warrant for your arrest on a charge of murder—and here it is. I'm asking you to accompany me, and I'll take full responsibility for whatever happens afterwards."

"If you do that, Inspector, you will lose your position on the Force. It would not be a happy moment for your wife and three children, would it?"

Brough visibly started. He flashed an amazed look at the Detective-Sergeant who was looking up blankly from his chair, a notepad on his knee.

"Who told you—"

"I see no reason to explain myself," Thomas Smith interrupted, "and I must ask you to leave. I'm not going to let you make a fool of yourself, inspector, because I don't intend to go with you,"

"I don't want to use force, sir," Brough said ominously. "But if I must, I must—"

He strode forward with the full intention of gripping Thomas Smith's arm, but instead he lurched wildly into mid-air, caught his foot in the rug, and then dropped onto his knees. He looked dazedly about him.

"What the blazes—!" he gasped. "Where'd he go?"

The Detective-Sergeant had jumped to his feet and was staring blankly about the empty room.

"He—he just vanished, sir! The moment you dived at him! He sort of went thin and I could see the furniture through him. Then—then he'd gone."

"Don't be a fool!" Brough yelled, getting on his feet. "How could any man do that? He jumped, or something—into the next room maybe, and you missed seeing him do it!"

Both men plunged immediately into the bedroom, the dressing room, and then the bathroom—but there was no sign of Thomas Smith. When they came back into the lounge they looked at one another uneasily.

"If I report this I'll be certified," Brough muttered. "All I can do to satisfy the high-ups is say that I couldn't get hold of Smith—which is true. Let's get back to the Yard and think out what we do next."

The moment they had departed Thomas Smith reappeared in the empty room and smiled to himself.

"Laws, laws, laws," he murmured. "Why is it that intelligent beings strangle themselves so with—"

He stopped as there was a light knock on the door. For a moment he hesitated and then he opened it. Glenda was in the corridor, her small Press-camera hidden away in her handbag.

"Well, Miss Carlyle!" Thomas Smith smiled down on her and waved a hand into the lounge. "A pleasant surprise indeed. Do come in."

Glenda did so, her expression half puzzled. When she was seated and the door closed again Thomas Smith came over and stood looking at her.

"Something troubling you?" he enquired.

"Yes. As I came into the hotel I saw Chief-Inspector Brough and a sergeant leaving: I know them pretty well. They didn't notice me. They seemed preoccupied about something. Am I right in thinking that they'd been to see you?"

"Quite right—but the interview was not too successful."

"You mean they didn't arrest you?"

"They didn't get around to that."

Glenda sighed. "I know Brough well. I've followed up the women's angle on several of the cases he's handled, and I have never known him to tackle anybody without being sure of his ground. What did he want—just an interview?"

"He came all prepared to arrest me, only—" Thomas Smith paused and smiled absently. "Only I think I convinced him that it would not be a wise move."

Glenda got up again quickly. "You don't mean you played one of your mental tricks on him, too? Made him forget, or something?"

"On the contrary I think he'll remember what happened in here only too well. I have, briefly, put him in the position that he does not know what to do. As I told you, I am well able to take care of myself. Anyway, none of this explains why you are here."

"You don't know? I thought you'd have worked it all out from my mind by now."

"I would rather you told me yourself."

"All right. I'm here because my editor wants a story about you—to match up, so he thinks, with your arrest. He also wants your photograph to run with the story."

Thomas Smith laughed and settled Glenda back in her chair again. Then he seated himself opposite her.

"Since I am not likely to be arrested, the story about me will not have much value, will it?"

"Believe me, Mister Smith, when I tell you I had no intention of ever writing a story in any way derogatory concerning you. How could I, after the wonderful thing you did for my mother today, after the wonderful gift you gave me for my trifling services? The story I was intending to write was one of your benevolence and miracle-working. A story that would prove that you could not possibly be the murderer Scotland Yard, my editor, and the general public are so willing to think."

"I am afraid, Glenda, that your journalistic power will be of no avail when the public wishes to think otherwise."

"You called me—Glenda," she said, after a moment.

"I hope you don't mind?" He smiled. "We are such good friends. Call me 'Thomas' if you like."

"I prefer 'Tom'. And 'Glenny' for myself."

He laughed. "So be it, Glenny. As I was saying—"

"No, hear me out," she insisted. "Don't you realize that you are the strangest man who ever walked back into civilization from—er—wherever you've been? Don't you realize that you can accomplish things no other person can? But to get back to cases. A story about your beneficence—particularly the story about my mother—would make yon safe from any murder charge. Nobody would condemn a man who can be so useful to the community."

"I have nothing further to add," Thomas Smith replied. "I wish I could explain— but I can't for many reasons."

Glenda took her notebook and pencil from her handbag. "I'll write the story here and now, then you can give it your blessing before I turn it in. Anything you don't want me to say can be deleted."

Thomas Smith nodded and Glenda began to write. When she had finished she read the report through in a deliberate voice and Thomas Smith remained silent, giving her all his attention. When it was finished she glanced up enquiringly and found him smiling. "I feel quite flattered," he laughed. "I'm still surprised that the information about my curing your mother can assume such importance. Yes, the article has my blessing and I hope your editor likes it."

"Concerning the bit about the diamonds," Glenda mused. "You can't add anything, I suppose? Explain where they came from or how it is you can produce them when you need them?"

"No, I can't add anything—but you can say that in my opinion, viewing things as a man who has been away for a long time, the community is hag-ridden with too many laws."

Glenda nodded and added the necessary notes. Then she fished in her bag and brought forth the small but efficient folding Press-camera.

"Just one photograph to go with the write-up," she said.

"I would much rather not." Thomas Smith's voice was very quiet and deliberate.

"Nearly everybody says that. Modesty, I suppose." The flashbulb glared momentarily and GIenda smiled. Thomas Smith sat looking at her and then he gave a sigh.

"I don't think that is going to be of much use to you, Glenny."

"That's my worry." Glenda put the camera back into her handbag. "Tomorrow's date still stands, I take it?"

"Of course." Thomas Smith rose. "I'll meet you at your place at ten."

Glenda returned to the *Clarion* offices as quickly as possible. Leaving her story with the news editor she went into the darkroom to develop the photograph she had taken. The result made her blink. With the print only just fixed and still wet she gazed at it in bewilderment—until a knock on the door made her turn.

"Safe to enter, Miss Carlyle?" asked a copy-boy. "The boss has sent me for a photograph."

"I'll bring it myself," Glenda replied, her voice faraway with incredulity. She opened the door and hurried into the news editor's office with the damp print in her fingers. The news editor gave her a grim look.

"What's this trash you've written about a murderer?" he barked.

"He's not a proven murderer yet, chief, and unless I'm crazy he never will be."

"There's every possibility that Thomas Smith will be under lock and key by tomorrow, or sooner. You don't suppose I can print this nonsense about a miracle-worker when that happens, do you?"

"It isn't nonsense: it's the truth. The woman he cured is my own mother, and she can verify it."

The news editor hesitated and then glanced at the limp print in Glenda's hand. "That his photo? Let's have it— For Pete's sake, what's this?"

Glenda said nothing and the news editor's eyes dropped back to the astonishing photograph in his hand. It depicted a suit of clothes by itself in an armchair, a reading lamp over the top left hand shoulder. At last the news editor looked up bleakly.

"Just what do you think you're doing, Glenny? First a story I can't use, and now a photograph which belongs in the trick photography section!"

"I photographed Mister Smith in exactly the same way as I'd photograph anybody else," Glenda snapped. "I just don't understand it! I told you he's a strange person."

"Strange he might be, but I refuse to believe that he is the invisible man'! This is no longer funny, Glenny! I've given you your chance and you've muffed it. Now Edwards had better take over." The switch on the desk-phone clicked. "Send in Edwards—with a camera."

"Look here," Glenda said desperately, "suppose I can prove to you that my mother had been given up by specialists as a hopeless arthritis case, and that now she is perfectly well?"

"For your mother's sake I'm glad to hear it—but we're not dealing with the better side of Thomas Smith. It's his worst side that interests us: the side of a murderer! That is the only thing the public is interested in, or will be when he's arrested."

"Hadn't you better make sure that he is arrested before printing anything about it?"

"You don't have to teach me my business!"

Snub-nosed, red-haired Edwards came in. He was probably the most cocksure reporter the *Clarion* had.

The news editor said: "Hop over to the *Zenith* Hotel, Edwards, and see Thomas Smith. Have an angle on him ready for when his arrest breaks—which might be at any moment—and get his picture."

"On my way," Edwards responded, and with that the news editor picked up the telephone. In a moment he was speaking to Chief-Inspector Brough.

"*Clarion* here, Inspector. How are things regarding Thomas Smith—? Huh?"

The news editor paused, listening.

"Dropping the case? But you can't! Something has come up? What, for instance?"

The news editor listened, his eyes infinitely astonished, then he began to protest again.

"But what sort of an excuse is that? There have been plenty of criminals the police couldn't get hold of—but this one is right in the *Zenith* Hotel for the picking up! You don't expect me to print that, do you? You—you what? You don't expect me to print anything? Now look here, Brough, you and I have co-operated too long for you to fob me off with that kind of a story. What's it all about? What's Thomas Smith done to get you Yard boys by the nose?"

When the news editor had the answer he compressed his lips. "All right, good-bye," he growled, and put the phone down.

"Well?" Glenda asked.

"For some reason I can't fathom, the Yard has decided to call off the case against Thomas Smith—at least for the time being."

Glenda left the office and returned to her desk in the main news-room. When after a while Edwards reappeared he was looking upset

"Enjoy yourself?" Glenda asked him, and he glared at her.

"Like hell! I got no story at all, but I think I got a photograph. I'm going to find out in the darkroom."

"I'll come with you," Glenda said quickly, following him.

And ten minutes later the news editor was looking at a damp print that showed a suit of clothes standing by itself in a comfortably furnished lounge. His color became dangerously red.

"So you're trying tricks too, Edwards, eh? What in blazes is this, anyway? First of April?"

"Now wait a minute, chief," Edwards implored. "I took that photo facing Smith, just the same as I am facing you now. I don't understand it—or perhaps I do," Edwards finished absently.

"You do?" The news editor's eyes narrowed. "Glenny here tried to take a photo and got the same invisible man effect. You haven't done any better, so what's the answer?"

"My guess is that he can become invisible whenever he wants. I may have seen things, and maybe I should be in the loony-bin, but I saw Thomas Smith disappear before my eyes! I asked him for a slant on why he murdered those two men. He said it was because they deserved it. When I asked him why the police hadn't picked him up, he said it was because of—this! And he just melted into thin air and vanished, clothes and all. I was left with my jaw on the carpet."

"Then?" the news editor asked, in a quiet voice.

"He reappeared, smiling like the Sphinx, and said it was going to be difficult for the law to catch a man like him. He also added that they were wrong in trying to do so since he had done no real harm in destroying two men who were not fit to live. I asked him how he knew they were not—apart from the crimes he had prevented in each case—and he said he knew the kind of minds they had, which sufficed."

Edwards gave a shrug, a baffled look in his eyes." While he was talking I just automatically got my camera focused and took a photo of him as he stood there. This is it. Smith just grinned when he knew I'd taken the picture and then showed me the door. I went—and I was glad to! He isn't a man chief. I—I don't know what he is!"

"Glenny, do you know what he is?" the news editor asked.

"No. That's straight, chief: I don't. He won't tell me. All I know of him is that he is a benefactor and that I'm closer to him than anybody, mainly because he saved me from assault. I probably know him better than anybody else, but he's still a stranger in our midst."

"But a stranger from where?" the news editor snapped. "That is what we must find out."

"I've been telling you that all along, chief," Glenda said patiently. "That's why I've written that story about him. I knew he would never be arrested because I know just how mysterious—how magical—his powers seem to be. You can have a scoop on this man if you want it. He has no objection. I have his word on that."

The news editor's eyes gleamed "A real invisible man! Mysterious healer in our midst! I see now why Brough isn't going any further! How can he if his quarry vanishes from under his nose? Brough didn't tell me that, but Edwards knows. Okay, I'll handle it that way. But I wish to heaven I had a photograph. Why not ask him why he doesn't appear in a negative, Glenny?"

"I'll see him tomorrow and I'll find out all I can," she promised.

Glenda left the office; then the news editor glanced at Edwards quickly.

"Okay, Edwards, that's all. Leave it to Glenny. If she can't get the gen nobody can."

*　*　*

Chief-Inspector Brough was seated in his office at Scotland Yard. In a corner at his own desk Detective-Sergeant Cavendish was browsing through the notes he had made at the interview with Thomas Smith—and getting exactly nowhere.

The chief Inspector had been seated at his desk for 20 minutes after his return from the *Zenith* Hotel, turning over every point in his mind, nor had his admission of failure over the phone to the news editor of the *Clarion* improved his temper.

"The thing's ridiculous!" he declared finally. "That fellow just couldn't have vanished into thin air! We were hypnotized into believing it, or something. That's the answer—just the same as he put the influence on Chantry about those diamonds."

"Then he must be a mighty strong hypnotist, sir," Cavendish commented morosely. "And we're neither of us what you might call the weak-willed type."

"Well anyway, the possibility of hypnotism is far more likely than of a man just vanishing, and I'm in an awkward spot . . . I'm supposed to arrest him, and if I don't, what sort of an explanation am I going to give? That our man does a disappearing act? I can see the Assistant Commissioner believing that one!"

Brough snapped on the desk-phone and asked Dr. Bell of the psychiatric division to step into his office. In a few moments Bell came. He had just been about to depart for home.

"Hope it's nothing urgent, Brough," he growled. "Look at the time!"

"I won't detain you any longer than I can help, doctor. Have a seat. I want a few details about those two men who were 'mentally murdered', so-called. What conclusion have you and the other experts arrived at?"

"I gave it all in my report," Bell replied, sitting down.

"But it doesn't tell me what I want to know. I've a job on my hands trying to nail down the mental killer. He has amazing powers—even to making himself invisible, or else hypnotizing the sergeant and myself into believing it."

"Sounds far-fetched," Bell commented. "Still, I suppose that a sufficiently powerful mind could make anybody believe anything. I have a theory about this Thomas Smith. Possibly he is from Tibet, or has been there and discovered things unknown to people of the western world. It would account for his magical powers, those diamonds you are worried about, and even his apparent disregard for human life."

"Yon mean Yogi stuff?"

"Something like it. If so he'll give you a run for your money!"

"He's done that already," Brough commented sourly.

"The whole business is uncanny," Dr. Bell declared. "Our examination of those two dead men showed that the conscious parts of their brains had been destroyed by some process which looks, at first sight, to be electrical. But the term 'electrical' might also be construed to mean 'vibrational,' which is more or less the same thing. What I mean is, the brain gives out vibrations. It gives it forth in much the same way as a radio transmitter gives out its waves. Anything in the vibratory field is basically electrical.

So, assuming we have a brain of extraordinary power it follows that it will emit vibrations of extraordinary force. Thus, such a brain might emit a force capable of destroying part of another brain of less power, just as one very powerful electrical transmitter can swamp a weaker one. In other words, I think that the brain of Thomas Smith is so strong that it can, by vibration, or mental power if you prefer, destroy the conscious area of another, lesser brain. From what we have learned, those two men did not die instantly. It happened some time after they left Thomas Smith. My guess on that is that he started some mentally corrosive process in the brains of both men which brought about their deaths soon afterwards."

"A pretty theory, but with no parallel in hard fact," Brough said skeptically.

"Neither has this man's queer gift of apparently making himself invisible at will. There is one thing you must understand, Brough. A brain of the highest possible development can accomplish almost anything. No such brain apparently exists in the human race, but it is not beyond possibility that one might turn up and be capable of all the things Thomas Smith seems capable of doing. In other words, he is a phenomenon who seems to have the mastery of mental science to the nth degree. But to prove such powers in a court of law, which concerns itself with facts, would be next to impossible. Something much more concrete is demanded."

"Such as? How does one even start to tackle a person like this?"

"That is your problem, Brough. I'm not a policeman."

Brough nodded moodily. "Thanks anyway. I don't need to detain you any further. I can grasp what you're driving at, even if it doesn't help me much."

At 10 o'clock the following morning Thomas Smith arrived at Glenda's flat. As she opened the door to him he greeted her cheerfully.

"Hello, Glenny! Ready?"

"Ready. Let's be on our way before my landlady spots us and asks awkward questions."

"More rules and regulations," Thomas Smith sighed. !I never saw a community more tied hand and foot."

"By the way, have you seen the *Clarion*?"

"With your story about me?" Thomas Smith laughed. "Yes, I've seen it. I think you are ascribing to me a lot of virtues I don't possess, Glenny."

"Not for a moment! You can't deny the miracle which cured my mother."

"I suppose," Thomas Smith mused, "it depends what one considers constitutes a miracle. For instance, for you to remove a stone from the pad of a dog's foot would seem like a miracle to the dog: to you it would be commonplace and natural! There, I think., we have the measure of the difference in our outlooks."

"But, Tom, you're a human being the same as I am! Why should our outlooks be so different?"

"You'll understand one day. In the meantime I have not the least doubt that you will remain loyal to me."

Glenda said little more until they were in the train for Bedford's Fold—where her home was situated—then she asked: "Are there any particular places you wish to see today or is it to be just a general run around?"

"We might go as far as the coast and back, taking your mother with us if she wishes to go."

"I hardly think she will," Glenda responded. "Sunday is the day when her friends come in."

Thomas Smith looked absently out of the compartment: window. "I suppose people don't sunbathe at this time of year?"

"Not unless they're crazy. Why?"

"To me, the cult of sunbathing is as baffling as smoking. I can see no sense in saturating oneself in ultra-violet radiation. What is the reason for it?"

"I think people imagine they look healthy when they're bronzed."

"What a fallacy! A man can look bronzed and be dying on his feet. What it amounts to is vanity!"

Glenda changed the subject, chiefly because she liked sunbathing herself in the summer months—when time allowed.

"I believe," she said, "that you had a visit from Edwards of the *Clarion* last night and did a vanishing act?"

"Yes. My sudden disappearance shocked him as much as it did Inspector Brough, I think."

"Since it's an accomplishment nobody has ever demonstrated before I can hardly wonder at that!"

"Yes, I suppose the fourth dimension is in the main purely theoretical, even to the cleverest mathematicians."

"So that's how you do it? The fourth dimension!"

"Naturally." Thomas Smith seemed satisfied with his casual explanation. "Three dimensions are very limiting. The fourth gives one limitless freedom, but of course one must thoroughly understand it."

"I can imagine!" Glenda felt and looked uncomfortable. "To me, who can hardly repeat the multiplication table, the fourth dimension is as far overhead as the sky. To understand it demands a genius, and to utilize it demands a—a mental giant. Which is exactly what you are!"

"If you wish it, Glenny," Thomas Smith smiled inscrutably.

"Why didn't you tell me you'd made yourself invisible when Brough came to see you? You merely said you had done something which would give him sleepless nights."

"It all struck me as so commonplace I didn't think to detail it. Now I realize it must have seemed a baffling trick."

"Where did you learn it? The same place where you found the diamonds?"

"Yes," Thomas Smith assented, but he did not elaborate. Instead he added: "I notice two things missing in most people. They don't seem to have their sixth-sense developed, and they live perpetually in three dimensions."

"All of which leads me to think that you are not of this world," Glenda said slowly. "No human being has ever had a developed sixth-sense, or any knowledge of the fourth dimension—save perhaps a few ancient seers and miracle workers." She mused over this, and then added hesitantly: You don't belong to a bygone age, do you? You're not a patriarch or somebody come to take a look at the modern word? You're not for instance the—the greatest miracle worker of them all whom the Christian world still worship?"

"No, I am not," Thomas Smith answered.

"Then who are you? I know you say you have been in the jungle somewhere, but somehow I don't believe that any more. Mysterious though jungle regions may be, and mighty though some of the secrets may be which are still hidden there, I don't think they could account for your baffling powers or the diamonds you can produce. Please, Tom, tell me before I go crazy!"

"I can't," he replied simply. "I've made that clear already. Not that I don't wish to, but I'm under orders and I must obey them."

Glenda started. "Great heavens, don't tell me you are under the dictate of somebody else! There couldn't be anybody cleverer than you, surely?"

"There could be—and there is."

"Oh!" Glenda sank into silence for a while. Then: "How is it you do not appear in a photograph?"

Thomas Smith gave his inscrutable smile. "I'll tell you why later—when I explain everything else."

Upon arrival at her home Glenda and Thomas Smith found her mother as well and cheerful as when they had left her the day before, and full of the information she had read in the *Clarion*.

"It's the first time I ever got myself into the news, Mister Smith!" she exclaimed, laughing. "I find it quite a moving experience."

"Hardly as moving as that of your recovery, I imagine," he commented.

"No. Nothing will ever equal my emotion when that happened. I still don't understand it." Mrs. Carlyle relaxed in thought for a moment, her eyes on the crocuses in the vase then she brisked up again. "Will you be staying for lunch, Glenny? You usually do on Sunday."

"Not this time, mum. Tom and I are going for a drive. You'll have your friends as usual, surely? You won't miss me?"

"I'll try not to," her mother smiled. "At least you will be in good hands."

So before very long Glenda and Thomas Smith were on their way to the local garage for the car, and Glenda took the wheel as before.

They had been traveling at a moderate speed for half-an-hour when Thomas Smith, who had his eyes on the rear view mirror, glanced behind him.

"I hardly think it can be coincidence that a black car is about a mile behind us," he said. "It's been at that distance ever since we left Bedford Fold."

Glenda peered at the image of the car behind and then frowned.

"No reason why it shouldn't be coincidence," she said. "This is the only road to the coast from Bedford's Fold."

"Pull up for a moment and we'll see if they pass us."

Glenda nodded and stopped the car. The following car did not become any larger. It, too, had stopped. Thomas Smith chuckled as he met the girl's surprise glance.

"Scotland Yard," he commented.

"Then they must have followed us from London!"

"Possibly I have been followed all the way from the *Zenith* Hotel. Considering the speed at which the local train moved our pursuers could easily have kept up with it by road, or else have driven ahead to Bedford's Fold to await us."

Glenda looked annoyed. "Which spoils everything!"

"Drive on," Thomas Smith ordered, "and turn off the first side-road you see."

Glenda obeyed and for five miles there was no break in; the road, then she spotted a narrow lane twisting away towards a farm. She turned into it, proceeded a hundred yards, and put on the brakes. Immediately Thomas Smith got out of the car and walked back to the main road. The black car came on and when it was close to him Thomas Smith stepped into view. The car stopped. It contained two plainclothes policemen in the front seat. The one who wasn't driving lowered his window and looked out.

"Go straight on, gentlemen," Thomas Smith said. "You have no interest whatever in Miss Carlyle and myself."

The man said nothing and wound the window up again. He gazed fixedly in front of him and his partner started the car once more. It continued straight on down the main road until it was lost to sight. Thomas Smith stood watching it, then turned as Glenda came running up to him.

"What in the world did you do to chase them off?" she exclaimed.

"I pointed out the uselessness of following us and suggested they should drive straight on."

"You mean yon gave them a mental order?"

"At least they have driven on. We'll not be troubled by them again, Glenny, so we might as well continue our tour."

They did so; and in the course of the morning—barring a. break at a wayside drive-in for refreshment—they covered most of the south coast between Folkestone and Bognor Regis.

CHAPTER FIVE
On trial for murder

In the time they had been together they had exchanged so much information—Glenda chiefly giving it—that she was in a complete daze as to what it had all been about. For instance, Thomas Smith had collected grass, filled a bottle with sea water at Bognor Regis, filled a bag with sand and small pebbles—and indeed had done everything to render the mystery of his personality and origin all the more obscure. Glenda had wondered about it all, as well she might, but had known better than to ask questions.

"This has been one of the most interesting days I have spent so far," Thomas Smith said, when the car had been garaged again and they were walking back to her home. "I am fully aware how puzzled you are, Glenny, and I appreciate your silence. You will be rewarded eventually."

Glenda paused in the darkness, the stars glittering high overhead in the frosty air.

"Before we go into the house," she said, "there are one or two things I want to ask you. I don't want to do it before mum: she doesn't understand this situation as well as I do."

"Ask anything you wish, Glenny. If I can't answer I'll say so."

"It's about my editor. He wants to run a series concerning you, very similar to the article that appeared today. I want your permission to write up everything we have done today."

Thomas Smith hesitated; then he spoke firmly. "I'm sorry, Glenny, but I can't give you permission to publicize my activities. I wish them to remain my secret—and yours."

"Very well," Glenda said, disappointed. "I'll respect your wishes."

It was upon her return to her London flat—having parted from Thomas Smith at the *Zenith* Hotel with the assurance that he would get in touch with her again shortly—that Glenda found Inspector Brough waiting outside her door. As she came to the top of the stairs he moved forward to greet her.

"Good evening, Miss Carlyle. I hope you don't mind my hanging about like this—"

"On the contrary," Glenda gave him a cold glance, "what do you suppose my landlady is going to think when I have a Scotland Yard officer waiting for me?"

"I told her I was a solicitor: that should suffice."

"Solicitor, on a Sunday? Really, Inspector!"

"I've got to have a few words with you," Brough continued earnestly. "About this chap Smith. It's plain from your article in the *Clarion* that you know more about him than anybody else does."

"Well, maybe I do." Glenda opened the door of her flat. "Come in, Inspector—" She switched on the light.

He followed her into the lounge, closing the door behind him. Glenda motioned to the chesterfield and then sat down opposite him.

"Without putting too fine a point on it, Inspector, you are licked, are you not?" she asked.

"Not altogether. Though I must admit that this mental marvel, or whatever he is, is giving me plenty of headaches. That is why I want your help."

"Then I'm afraid you are not going to get it. I have a great respect for Mister Smith and will certainly not take sides against him."

"You know, of course, that he is a murderer? No mention of that appears in your article about him, but I assume you are acquainted with all the facts."

"I know every detail about them—except the method of killing. However, the elimination of two vile men weighs as nothing to me against Mister Smith's curing of my mother. She was the woman referred to in my article."

"Listen," Brough said intently. "Let's get this into proper focus. I can well believe that you are overawed by this man's extraordinary personality, but the fact does remain that he has broken the law and must be called to account. I have tried to arrest him and failed—"

"Because he became invisible. I heard about that."

Brough grimaced. "I then decided to set two plainclothes men to watch him. They did so up to a point, discovering in the process that he owns—or you own—a very expensive car in which you career around the country-side. Then, those two men were ordered away from their duty—and obeyed! They have a story about mental compulsion, which, knowing the queer personality of Smith, I am prepared to believe. However, I am satisfied that you and Smith are very close, so much so that you might find yourself cited as an accessory."

Glenda laughed. "That's impossible! Stop trying to throw scares into me, Inspector."

"If it's the only way to get you back to a sense of civic responsibility I'll try it!" he retorted. "Let me tell you that I am not satisfied about the source of Smith's diamonds," Brough continued inexorably. "You are as mixed up in it as he is, and if we ever get as far as a law court you'll be dragged in. That car, for instance. The salesman says you chose it and Smith bought it as a present. A twenty-five thousand pound present is a mighty big one!"

"No law against giving presents," Glenda said.

"Unless they can be interpreted as hush-money."

"Hush-money!" Glenda looked indignant. "Concerning what?"

"Theft, and maybe murder!" Brough retorted. "Perhaps crimes of which you are aware but which, so far, the law is not." Then as Glenda remained silent Brough got to his feet. "Very well, Miss Carlyle, but take my tip—you're playing a damned dangerous game, trailing around with a man like this. I have to warn you that if you keep on doing it you'll be dragged down with him, when we get him."

"When!" Glenda emphasized. "In the meantime I can assure you that my car has nothing to do with hush-money, nor do I know of any crime connected with Mr. Smith's diamonds. He happens to like me, and I like him. A present is quite a natural sequence under such conditions, isn't it?"

Brough shrugged. "Okay, Miss Carlyle, if that is the way you want it. I just hoped you might have preferred to be sensible."

With that he took his departure and Glenda was left to think matters over to herself.

The next day she did not see or hear from Thomas Smith and the fact worried her.

Many letters were coming into the *Clarion* office concerning him, most of the writers wishing to know where he could be found, and if he would attend this or that function and cure people whom medical science had pronounced incurable, and the city editor rang the *Zenith* Hotel to speak to him about the inquiries. The reply he got surprised him, and he called Glenda in.

"Where's Smith?" he asked.

"At his hotel, Chief, as far as I know."

"He's checked out, and didn't say where he was going. He didn't tell you?"

"All he said was that he would get in touch with me. I can't understand why he should leave like that."

"The reception clerk tells me that the hotel is swarming with people wanting to see Smith. No doubt he foresaw what would happen and left before many arrived."

Somewhat dazed, particularly as he had left no forwarding address, Glenda returned to her desk. Then a thought occurred to her. She picked up the phone and called Inspector Brough at the Yard.

"Yes, I'm aware he has checked out," Brough said. "Where he is I don't know."

"You'd have him watched," Glenda said. "Do me a favor, Inspector. If you find out where he is please let me know."

"Why should I? You haven't helped me so far."

"Forget you're a policeman for the moment, Inspector, and be a human being. I just don't know how I'll live without Mr. Smith."

"He certainly has a hold over you. Hasn't he? All right. If I hear anything I'll ring you."

"Thanks." Glenda rang off, frowning as she struggled to assimilate the situation. Then she saw a copy-boy staggering to her desk with a square wooden box cradled in his arms.

"For you," he announced, dumping it. "It came by special messenger."

Glenda, on opening the box found an expensive new laptop. A note was trapped saying: "**MANY HAPPY RETURNS OF TOMORROW**".

She had no need to ask herself who had sent it. She searched the box for some clue as to Thomas Smith's whereabouts but failed to discover a single hint. Slowly her worry began to return.

About that moment Thomas Smith was buying a large country house between London and Bedford's Fold, a house he had seen as standing abandoned on his trip from the city to Glenda's home. It had extensive grounds, the nearest neighbor was three miles distant, and the place, falling into disuse, was going relatively cheaply.

It was not that Thomas Smith had any need to consider money. He liked the loneliness of the place and bought it. Then he spent the remainder of the day having the place furnished by a London firm. The priority he demanded meant higher cost, but this he brushed aside.

Even so it was three days before he had the place passably tidied up and furnished. During the nights he did not trouble to sleep. He spent his time in one or the other of the untidy, jumbled rooms, sitting thinking hour after hour, apparently regardless of the January cold. When he needed a meal he ate several tablets from a small container he always carried.

Not far from the house, enduring the inclemency of the weather, two Scotland Yard men kept constant watch. They had trailed their quarry from London—he having made no effort to conceal his movements—and had reported back to Brough about the purchase of Baynton Hall by the mystery man.

On the fourth evening, just after the winter dark had settled down, Thomas Smith emerged from the house. The two waiting plainclothesmen hidden in laurel bushes watched him as he walked to the railway station. He boarded a local train for London and they, too, did likewise.

Thomas Smith did not alight until Victoria was reached. He walked off along busy main streets, branching presently into a dimly-lighted vista— and not very far behind him two plainclothes men patiently dogged him. Judging from the direction the stranger was taking, the men assumed that he was heading for Glenda's flat—then, abruptly, as they entered another long, dark street, something happened.

Ahead, clearly visible in the lamplight, there were a man and a woman. The woman screamed and the man swung up his arm. There was the momentary glitter of a knife-blade, but before it could descend Thomas Smith sprang forward and knocked the man sprawling.

"You'd better go," Thomas Smith said, glancing at the startled, flashily-dressed girl staring at him.

"He meant to kill me," she said breathlessly. "He told me to meet him here, and then he tried to knife me."

"Go—whilst you're safe."

The girl turned and ran. The man on the ground, still holding his knife, scrambled to his feet and flung himself forward savagely. Thomas Smith was ready for him. His right hand flashed up, twisted the knife from the man's grasp, and then brought the blade down.

With a gasping cry the man dropped, the knife buried to the hilt in his breast. Kneeling, Thomas Smith looked down at him—then he glanced round as the two plainclothes men came hurrying out of the gloom.

Thomas Smith stood up and waited. One of the plainclothes men took a look at the sprawled body and then turned.

"No doubt about it this time, Mister Smith," he said. "You knifed this man and killed him. My colleague and I saw you."

"You could hardly fail to. I assume you were following me?"

"Correct. All the way from that mansion you've bought in the country. I must ask you to accompany us to headquarters. My colleague will remain here with the body until a squad-car arrives with a doctor and divisional inspector."

The plainclothes man knew of Thomas Smith's magical vanishing act and was scared of the same thing happening again. It did not, however. Thomas Smith appeared quite resigned to his fate.

The first plainclothes man made a telephone call and some 20 minutes after killing the man who had tried to stab the unknown girl, Thomas Smith found himself in Brough's office at Scotland Yard.

"Good work, Stacey," he said to the man who had brought Smith. "I didn't get a full report over the telephone. Let's hear what you have to say."

In detail the policeman explained, and the chief inspector made notes on his scratch-pad. Then, when Stacey had left the room, Brough said, as Cavendish took notes:

"Now Mister Smith, it's time we had a chat. On the occasions when you disposed of that tramp and Henry Armstrong you did it without laying a finger on them; and when I questioned you at the hotel you made yourself invisible. This time, however, you have killed with a knife and been seen doing it by two responsible men, which is all the evidence I want—and further you have not made any effort to escape, either by invisibility or any other method. Why?"

"I have no wish to disappear. I prefer to go through with this trial and once and for all put an end to this nuisance of being hounded and followed. To keep escaping—easy though it is to me—is not the right answer. I thought at first that it was, but I underestimated your tenacity. The better way is to be acquitted by a court and leave the way clear for the future. I have much to do and I want to be unhampered by the law trying to condemn me as a criminal."

"Then you think you can be proven innocent?"

"I have no doubt of it. I remain convinced that wherever I have killed the community has gained. This evening I happened by accident on that man who was trying to stab that girl. I killed him because it was the logical thing to do. The girl herself had done nothing to merit his villainy. He, on the other hand, was filled with nothing except the desire to destroy her."

"How do you know that?" Brough demanded.

"By the same process that I know your wife's birthday is a fortnight from today and that you are wondering whether or not to buy her a new washing-machine."

The Chief-Inspector gave a grim smile. "That thought-reading trick again, eh? I don't doubt that it has a logical explanation really, the same as your invisibility stuff which I believe to be basically hypnotic. You'll find it a different thing trying to hypnotize a judge and jury and a courtroom full of people!"

* * *

Committed for trial, Thomas Smith did not seem any the more disturbed than he had been from the first. He accepted everything with good temper. His only visitor from the outer world, apart from his lawyer, was Glenda, and as often as the law permitted she spent a few moments with him.

"Honestly, Tom, I think you're doing everything possible to make your chances worse!"

"Why?" He smiled at her across the table in the guarded brick wall room in which they sat.

"Well, for one thing, who is this defense counsel you have engaged? David Dyson. He's only a struggling young lawyer and can't possibly handle a case as complicated as this. With the money you have at your command you can employ the finest legal brains."

"I don't need them, Glenny. David Dyson needs to win a complicated case to make a reputation. He is a deserving young struggler, so I'm giving him the chance."

Glenda made a helpless movement. "But he can't possibly win, Tom!"

"Don't worry Glenny: I know exactly what I am doing. I intend to put a stop to this law-chasing business."

For a moment Glenda was silent, then she said: "Why did you depart so suddenly without telling me anything?"

"I left the *Zenith* hotel for two reasons—one, because so many people might come chasing after me, of which fact you had already warned me when you referred to hero-worship; and also because I could not indulge certain private activities at the hotel. So I left. I did not tell you where I had gone because I wanted my new residence nicely prepared before you came to it. When I got it to rights I came immediately to London to tell you. I could have done it by phone, of course, but I preferred to see you. However, I finished up here, so I was not able to come and tell you as I had intended . . . When the trial is over I want you to come and see my new home. It's beautiful, and wonderfully private."

* * *

In due course the trial came. Glenda was subpoenaed as a witness and not, as the Chief-Inspector had hinted, as an accessory. When called upon to give her evidence she answered every question with a logical truthfulness, which astonished even herself. There was no question the prosecution counsel could put to her but what she had the exact answer ready, and more often than not she cut the ground from under his feet and left him wondering from what angle to strike next.

Then Mrs. Carlyle spoke also, and nothing could budge her from her gratitude to Thomas Smith for the freedom from ill-health which he had given to her. She set the court on its ears when she referred to the crocuses being as still as fresh as the day she had picked them. Mrs. Armstrong also gave evidence and no amount of trickery or cross-questioning could make her admit that she was sorry her husband was dead. She even left behind her the implication that Thomas Smith had killed in self-defense. One by one the witnesses paraded—

All those involved with Thomas Smith took their places on the stand—the police, the psychiatric and medical experts, David Chantry, the car salesman who had sold the £25,000 car, the estate agent who had sold to Thomas Smith a country mansion by the name of Baynton Hall, the negotiations for which had occupied him during the week he had been absent. And lastly, the widow of the man whom Thomas Smith had knifed. She, like Mrs. Armstrong, was not at all distressed at losing her brutal husband.

Throughout the proceedings, Thomas Smith sat motionless in the dock, his dark, magnetic eyes following each witness in turn, or else studying the varying expressions on the prosecuting counsel's face.

It all had a one-sided flavor, as though by some mysterious twist Thomas Smith was being proved a benefactor instead of a criminal.

Thomas Smith waited calmly while the Attorney General made his charge to the jury, which was followed by that of the Chief Justice. Then came the recess, that period—for Glenda at least—of agonizing waiting until the moment should come when the verdict would be given.

She was not allowed to see Thomas Smith, of course, but she was with him in spirit nonetheless. Has she seen him quite unmoved in an anteroom with warders guarding him, she would have felt less anguished in mind. He was even wearing that strange smile which the warders found so baffling. They had never seen a man smile like that before whilst awaiting a verdict.

Then the jury filed back into the courtroom and the Chief Justice returned to his position, and waited. Within the space of a few minutes it was all over and "Not Guilty" hummed along the wires from the central criminal court to dozens of newspapers.

Some of those in the court sat open-mouthed, others cheered. Thomas Smith, the miracle man, was free—and he walked out of the court smiling inscrutably, Glenda hanging onto his arm as they tried to dodge the people who thronged urgently around.

To their surprise a big car was waiting for them outside the court, and when motioned to it by a gray-suited man within, they gladly took refuge. The door was closed by a chauffeur and the car moved away.

Thomas Smith and Glenda looked at their rescuer . . . he was about sixty, well-built, florid, immaculately dressed, with sharp gray eyes.

"Why, you're Mr. Denroy!" Glenda exclaimed, in sudden recognition. "Alvin Denroy of Amalgamated Metals!"

"Right," he agreed. "I'm glad you decided to accept my hospitality and step into the car. I thought you might get tangled up. I had the idea from the way things were going that you'd be proven innocent, Mr. Smith, so I decided to have my car wait for you."

"Very kind of you," Thomas Smith said, shaking hands.

"Sooner or later, Mister Smith, you and I are going to have a little chat together," Denroy explained. "No reason why what we should not start to get acquainted, and then have our chat later, eh?"

"Yes—of course." Thomas Smith had a slight hesitation, as though he were trying to weigh up the situation. "At the moment I haven't time for a prolonged discussion, I'm afraid."

"That can come later. When you have some free time after resting from this harrowing trial, just get in touch with me at Amalgamated Metals. I fancy we can do each other a lot of good, Mr. Smith."

"You do?" Thomas Smith gave his inscrutable smile. Very well, I'll do that. Meanwhile, perhaps you wouldn't mind dropping us at Victoria?"

"By all means."

Brief though the meeting with the industrialist had been it had left an impression on Glenda. She was still thinking about it when, with Thomas Smith, she was on the train bound for Bedford's Fold. Her story had been 'phoned to the *Clarion*, and with her editor's blessing she was taking time out to try and learn more about Thomas Smith, or so she had said. Just for the moment she was content to sit back happily and absorb the glorious fact that the law had freed him—albeit mysteriously—and that they were together again.

"I shouldn't trust Alvin Denroy too much, Tom," she said presently.

"I have no intention of doing so, Glenny. In fact he's the type of whom I shall definitely be wary. If he wants me I'm afraid he'll have to come to me. I shall certainly not run after him."

"He won't come to you. He's too important."

"I'm not exactly weak myself," Thomas Smith smiled. "And I daresay I could match his money if that has to be the issue."

Glenda laughed. "I keep forgetting just how much money and power you have got, chiefly because you're so unassuming. Denroy, on the other hand, simply exudes authority, power, and—"

"Malice," Thomas Smith finished and there was something about the way he said it that stopped the conversation dead.

Glenda started on a fresh track. "I suppose we should have waited for mother at Victoria—but still, we had no idea how long she'd be. Never mind; we'll have everything ready for when she gets home."

"I'd planned to go to my new place, Glenny—three stops before Bedford's Fold. I want you to see it. Maybe it would be better, though, to go to your home first, pick up the car, and then drive back to Baynton Hall. Incidentally, I bought the mansion so that I could be equidistant from either your London flat or your cottage in Bedford's Fold. That way I don't feel quite so lonely."

Glenda looked at him seriously. "You are lonely, Tom, aren't you?"

"Lonely indeed." He gave a sigh and looked out of the window. "I can't measure the depth nor the breadth of it. Without you beside me I think I would . . . " He stopped, leaving a big interrogation mark at the end of his sentence.

"By rights," Glenda said after a while, "you should never have gotten away with it at the trial. It just seemed that everything went right for you—The statements I made, the uncertainty of the Attorney General—a most unusual thing for him—the conviction behind the words of the witnesses, the unanimity of the jury. It was though a charm were at work in the courtroom. I could sort of sense it. Not, mind you, that I don't think you deserved to be acquitted."

"They could not help but pronounce me innocent," he said, musing. "That was why I went through the trial, to put a stop to the law constantly pursuing me. Hereafter I am free, and if by some chance I see fit to eliminate others and am again brought to trial I shall again be proven innocent until at last the law gives up trying to convict me."

"It might not work a second time," Glenda warned.

"It would, my dear." Thomas Smith turned his head and looked at her steadily. "You spoke as you did in the courtroom and everybody else behaved as they did, because they could do nothing else. I held each of their minds in turn and told them exactly what to say. And they did. I find most minds, even the so-called cleverest, put up no resistance whatsoever."

"You mean you were acquitted because you used hypnosis?"

"Yes, if I had failed to accomplish my purpose I could always have disappeared, but this time I preferred legal release."

Glenda stared at him. But he said no more. As on other occasions he seemed to take his extraordinary powers for granted, and did not enlarge upon them.

Then presently, nodding through the window he exclaimed: "Look! There is my home, through the trees there! Like it?"

Glenda gazed at a massive pile set well back in its own grounds; then she began to nod eagerly. "It's beautiful, Tom! And probably even more beautiful inside. You've had an annex added, haven't you?" As the train continued on its way it gave a view of the side of the old mansion and a structure that was obviously new brick.

Yes. It's a sort of—laboratory. I've some experiments to make."

"Not dangerous ones, I hope!" Glenda protested.

"No. Would it matter if they were?"

"Of course it would!" Glenda's eyes met his frankly. "I just can't

141

imagine my world without you. It's not like falling in love. It's something else."

"You should try and overcome it," he replied seriously. "Our association can never be anything more than deep friendship."

"Of course," Glenda continued, "having never been impressed by any man until I met you I may well be a stranger to love when it has arrived. I only know that I somehow cannot picture my life without you. I'm afraid I have always been prosaic enough to think of love as another name for physical attraction, but in your case it isn't that which fascinates me. It's your entire personality, your tremendous power. If you were to get as far as asking me to marry you I'd say 'Yes' immediately. Perhaps not so much because I want to but because I couldn't think of saying 'No'."

"It is disturbing sometimes to dominate the mind of another, and not wish to," Thomas Smith replied. "That is all it is in your case, Glenny. I am a compelling, unavoidable influence, without wishing to be—and it isn't fair to you. I shall never ask you to marry me though. You may as well know that now."

Glenda could not help the despondency that crept into her expression. To her, this statement implied that one day he would step out of her life and leave an emptiness that she knew could never be filled. Married to him she could feel sure that he would be at her side.

"You mean you don't feel towards me as I do towards you?" she asked.

He looked troubled for a moment. "It isn't a question of that, Glenny. I'm extremely fond of you—as you know—and if it were possible I would ask you to marry me—but I just can't."

"You're married already perhaps?"

"No." Thomas Smith brooded. "No, it isn't that."

"Then what else can there be?" Glenda asked, puzzled.

"Between you and me, Glenny, there is an absolute barrier and neither of us can cross it. It just happens that we are attracted to each other and yet can do nothing about it. For you it is difficult to understand this attraction: for me the answer is plain. Some day I hope I shall make you understand."

Because she could think of nothing to say Glenda just gazed in bewilderment, noting the signs of mental struggle that were registered on his face. He did not explain further then however, and by the time they reached Bedford's Fold he seemed to have decided to let the matter drop.

*   *   *

Hardly speaking a word they went to Glenda's home and prepared a meal in readiness for the arrival of Mrs. Carlyle.

Once or twice Glenda wondered what the neighbors would be thinking, having seen her arrive with Thomas Smith; then he himself interrupted her thoughts with a grave comment.

"It doesn't matter what they think, Glenny. Remember what I told you. Act as you consider right and take no notice of anybody else."

"It isn't so easy when there are conventions and laws," Glenda sighed. "It would be different if we were engaged. Nobody could say a thing then. As it is I'll have a good deal of talking to do to explain my conduct. Serves me right. I should have waited for mother."

"Engaged," Thomas Smith repeated, musing. "To become engaged would mean marriage later. Otherwise, to make you comfortable, I would become engaged to you, but it would not be right if I did it without ever intending to marry you, would it?"

"Look here, Tom, haven't I been your friend for long enough by now to merit your entire confidence?" she snapped. "I keep on tolerating your strange remarks and utterly impossible questions, but I'm coming to the end of my patience. I've told you I'm fond of you—and I am. But please don't go on expecting me to be baffled indefinitely."

He smiled. "Your reaction is quite natural. I'm surprised you have been quiet about it for so long."

"Then tell me the facts! Who are you, and what is your business here? I won't publish it. I won't tell a soul. I just want to satisfy myself and know what kind of a man I'm a slave to."

Thomas Smith hesitated, seemed on the verge of explaining himself—and then he looked up as the main door suddenly opened and Mrs. Carlyle came in. Glenda slowly relaxed, fighting back her disappointment at the interruption. By the time she had turned to her mother she had forced a welcoming smile.

"So you got here ahead of me?" Mrs. Carlyle asked, kissing Glenda gently and then glancing at the laid table. "And a celebration tea all set out! Hello, Tom," she added shaking hands as he smiled at her. "Congratulations— Not that anybody in their right senses would have convicted you anyway."

"I'm glad you've decided to use my first name," he said.

"Time I did, isn't it? I think of you in the same way as I think of Glenny—as though you're a son of mine."

143

"It isn't quite that way, mum," Glenda said, "and it makes it awkward. Tom and I are not engaged, and we never will be."

"Why not? What is there against it?"

"A great deal," Thomas Smith answered. "Something Glenny and I cannot alter. I may be able to explain one day, but I can't at this moment."

"Oh, I see—" Mrs. Carlyle frowned. It was perfectly clear she did not see. "Then if you don't intend to become engaged to Glenny why do you keep on associating with her? It's all wrong, you know."

"Why?" he asked.

"Why? Well, because—er—" Mrs. Carlyle made a bewildered movement. "Because it just isn't done, that's why. No decent man keeps constant company with an un-married woman unless he intends to make her his wife, or unless she's a relative."

"Then let us say that I am a relative."

"But you're not!" Glenda objected, staring. "No relative at all. A complete stranger."

"I wonder. You too will wonder one day. For the time being we shall remain just friends."

Mrs. Carlyle half opened her lips to comment and then she met Thomas Smith's eyes. She knew in that moment that further argument was useless, and so did Glenda. She saw that Thomas Smith was looking at her, smiling in that odd way he had, and she knew more than ever that she must remain at his side for as long as he wished it. Her eyes strayed from his features to the crocuses on the table. They made a dappling of brilliance in the cold winter sunlight. They were still as fresh as the moment when her mother had picked them.

That evening Glenda drove herself and Thomas Smith to his new home, where she spent an awe-stricken hour wandering through the opulence of the great place and marveling at the speed with which everything had been fixed up. And elsewhere a meeting was in progress at the residence of industrialist Alvin Denroy.

In his library the cigars were fragrant, the wine superb, and as usual Denroy was doing all the talking. His three colleagues—'Oil' Brookings, 'Transport' Kendal, and 'Aircraft' Glosser were all listening and glancing at each other significantly at intervals.

"I tell you, gentlemen, this is the most wonderful thing that ever happened," Denroy insisted. "Nobody seem to have realized just how wonderful, except for a few of the fools who look on Thomas Smith as a

144

divine healer or something. That angle is of no interest to us, of course. Our concern is that he is a natural telepathist and a brilliant man in every way. I think, if he wished, he could rule the world."

The remaining three tycoons nodded somberly.

"Since we, unfortunately, because of human limitations, cannot rule the world," Denroy continued, "I think it would be to our advantage to secure the services of somebody who can."

"And give him the opportunity to do so?" asked the oil magnate. "Not for me, Al, thank you."

"I put it badly," Denroy apologized. "What I mean is, we should make it worth the while of this genius to read the thoughts of certain people for us! I don't have to tell you how valuable it would be to us to know, for instance, just what certain statesmen and leaders are planning to do at this moment. We could anticipate everything and amass even greater fortunes from that very knowledge alone."

"True," agreed the aircraft king, "but can this man be bought? I get the impression that he is wealthy, even as wealthy as we are, and judging from his statements can become trebly wealthy and at any moment he wishes. What offer could you make to a man like that?"

The industrialist examined the end of his glowing cigar and then said dryly: "I'm going to offer him the world!"

"Talk sense!" the transport king protested.

"It is sense, Kendal—believe me. I've heard enough about this man to have guessed long ago that his ambition is to master the world; but for some reason, brilliant though he is in his statement, he does not seem to know how to go about it. We could show him—or I could—in return for certain favors. In that way he'll be content, and so shall we. If, when our own ambitions are satisfied, he should prove a nuisance by being in too dominant a position, we can always take care of the situation."

"For my part," said the oil man, musing, "I should go very warily, Al."

"Warily?" Denroy laughed shortly. "You don't suppose I'm going to put on kid gloves to handle a fellow of 27 or so, do you—even if he is a phenomenon?"

The oil man insisted: "I'm as aware as you are of this man's prowess, as much as I'm aware that he is the strangest man as ever rose to power. That being so, I refuse to believe that anybody with such exceptional talents does not know how to go about ruling the world. The answer is that he does not want to! He probably has other plans."

"To a man who has exceptional power the mastery of others is the only possible end," Denroy retorted. "Anyway, I'm going to get him to help us."

"Apparently," the aircraft man said, "he is a clever telepathist and also has unusual ways of destroying people he doesn't like. What's going to happen if he manages to read your inner purposes? You won't be too safe, will you?"

"Naturally, there will be risks," Denroy admitted. "One cannot put over anything big without that possibility—but I'm prepared for it all. I'm getting Smith here and will get all the help I can from him. I shall want you boys to help lend some conviction. It may be more than I can handle alone."

The three glanced at each other and then with mutual assent they nodded.

"When does the interview come off?" Kendal asked.

"No idea as yet. I'll tell you the moment I've fixed it. I've already made a point of breaking the ice with Smith, and he's quite an agreeable young man who doesn't seem to know how powerful he really is. Our biggest trouble will probably not come from him, but from Glenda Carlyle of the *Clarion*."

"The one who writes those articles about him?" asked the oil man. "Shouldn't be difficult to keep her in her place, surely?"

"No, probably not," Denroy admitted, "but the trouble is that she knows only too well that we are not exactly saints and, being as close to Smith as she is, she may warn him to be on his guard. So we'll have her opposition to break down first. If the girl should prove too embarrassing to our plans we can always arrange something."

And at that moment Glenda was in the huge lounge of Baynton Hall. There was luxurious quietness around her. A fire was burning crisply in the old-fashioned grate, giving forth the only light there was and submerging the more remote corners of the room in deep shadow. Outside, the January afternoon had died and here and there a flake or so of snow drifted.

Glenda was happy. She had never been so happy in her life before. She was alone in this great, magnificently-appointed house with Thomas Smith. He was seated on a low chair opposite her, staring fathoms deep into the flames.

"In spite of sounding monotonous," Glenda said at last, "I still don't understand it."

Thomas Smith roused himself. "What this time, Glenny?"

"This magnificent place you have fitted up. What's the idea of it when it is purely for your own use? You are not a selfish, self-centered man, so why all this?"

"I believe one should have the best of everything."

Glenda looked at him intently, her violet eyes seeming black in the firelight.

"Tom, at the risk of going back over old ground, why can't I share things with you?"

"You can, for as long as you wish."

"I mean as your wife. It isn't that I want just to live in this house. I want to be near you. Why do you make me so attached to you only to frustrate me?"

He hesitated for a long moment, then getting out of the chair he came over and stood before her. "Stand up, Glenny," he requested, and she did so. The next thing she knew his arms were about her and he kissed her twice with possessive power. Then he stood back a little, still holding her shoulders, and looked down into her face.

"What extraordinary power a woman can exert over a man," he mused. "Even without conscious effort she can do it. It is something transcending all other dominations."

Glenda gave a wistful smile. "It's a pity you have to go all biological about it, Tom. For a moment I thought you had really come down to earth. Now you seem to be trying to find an excuse for having kissed me. You needn't you know. I liked it. I'd like it again, any time you want. We can't go on forever holding each other at arms' length. My whole life, everything, is tied up in you and whatever you do."

"I shouldn't have done that. Please don't interpret too much into those kisses, Glenny."

"Listen, Tom," she burst out impulsively, "when two people love each other as devotedly as we do they—"

She would have said a good deal more only she noticed that he was not even looking at her. He had gone back to his chair, his eyes fixed on the fire. She waited for a moment, then with a sigh she turned away and wandered across the room.

Before she fully realized it, lost as she was in her own moody thoughts, she had reached the dark expanses of the old-fashioned hall. There was no sound save the soft sigh of a northerly wind about the ancient eaves . . .

Against the stained glass windows the twilight still lingered, and tiny blurred ghosts of snow drifted.

Glenda shivered a little. Away from the fire the air was cold, but she wanted to think, to be alone for a moment, to try and decide for herself what she must do about Thomas Smith. She had no conscious idea of where she was going. In a house so huge it was like walking about out-doors. She only came to a halt when she realized from the smell of the atmosphere that she had come to somewhere different. The inescapable odor of age-old timbers had gone.

Instead there was the tang of newly-sawn wood and fresh paint. She reached out her hand and fumbled for an electric light switch. When the glow came into being she saw she was standing just inside the recently-built annex.

The place was filled with the most amazing radio equipment she had ever seen. Wondering, she walked forward slowly, looking about her in the bright light. She had seen, radio-transmitting stations before, but for complication none of them had been the equal of this one. She had common scientific knowledge enough to identify such details as trans-formers, and so forth—but here was equipment that baffled her.

She listened to the hum of power coming from behind a massive door, then she looked overhead at curiously-fashioned spiral antennae looped into the high ceiling. The windows were of frosted glass to negate all chance of anybody prying from outside.

Frowning to herself she strolled over to a desk, which, in design, reminded her of a giant typewriter or the manual of an organ. In a little well in the center was a chair screwed to the rubber-sheathed floor. Sitting in the chair she contemplated the scribbling-pad at her right elbow. A few words had been written upon it—

" . . . faced with a difficult situation. Must either ask for release from obligations so I can explain; or return home and bring the disturbing influence to an end. Have greatly underestimated the power of physical attraction which is not nearly so over-mastering at home, perhaps because we are schooled to rule our emotions."

Glenda read the words again, trying to make some sense out of them, then at a slight sound she turned. Thomas Smith had come into the annex and was standing looking at her. He was not smiling, neither was he angry. He just gazed, with so fixed a stare that Glenda felt her nerves quivering. For the first time in their association she felt vaguely afraid of him.

"How did you get in here, Glenny?" he asked levelly, coming forward.

"Oh, just by chance. The door was unlocked and so I wandered in." Glenda got quickly to her feet, feeling that she must keep talking. "You have a wonderful laboratory here Tom! Why didn't you show it to me when you took me over the house?"

"Because I didn't see what advantage it could be to you to see it."

"But that's absurd! It's the most wonderful place I have ever been in. I don't pretend to understand what the stuff is for, of course, or the first thing about it, but I'm sure it's something tremendously exciting and complicated."

"Complicated, yes," he agreed, and his gaze traveled to the notepad beside the chair. "You read that, I suppose?" he asked shortly.

"Yes, but I didn't understand it."

Glenda no longer felt that fear which had seized her for a moment. Thomas Smith did not appear angry. If anything he seemed undecided, so Glenda seized her chance.

"Tom, you don't belong to this world, do you?" she asked, her gaze fixed on him intently.

He raised his eyes to look at her and waited.

"Such a thought would have been too utterly fantastic to commence with," she hurried on, "but now I've come to see it is the only possible explanation. You don't know a thing about our customs; you're used to a social-order quite different from ours, and you have an intelligence far exceeding anything we of this world ever had—save perhaps the Ancients. You have also spoken of a barrier between us. So adding everything up there is only one conclusion: You do not belong to Earth! Am I right?"

"Not entirely," he answered, smiling—and Glenda frowned.

"In what sense do you mean that? You either do, or do not, surely?"

Glenda had no chance to discover whether he intended to answer, for at that moment there was the sound of a telephone ringing somewhere in the house. Thomas Smith reached forward and took her arm.

"We can talk elsewhere than in here," he said, and led her out of the laboratory, locking it behind him. Then he switched on the hall lights and went over to the telephone.

"Mister Smith?" asked a chesty voice.

"Speaking."

"Remember me? Alvin Denroy? I thought I'd like a word with you."

"Yes I recall you mentioning it, Mister Denroy." Thomas Smith's eyes strayed to Glenda and he saw her expression change at the mention pf the industrialist's name.

"How about a get-together?" Denroy asked.

"Might I ask for what purpose? I'm very busy."

At the other end of the wire Denroy scowled for a moment. He was not accustomed to being addressed so brusquely. Nevertheless it paid him to keep his tone amiable.

"It is a matter of great importance to both of us, Mister Smith, which I wish to discuss with you. Your recent activities have made you very important, and I myself am not exactly a nonentity, so—"

"You know where I live, Mister Denroy, if you wish to see me," Thomas Smith said briefly. "The address is Baynton Hall, Middle Bedford Fold, Sussex—a fact of which you must be aware since you have discovered my telephone number, not yet in the directory."

"When I take an interest in somebody I have all manner of people working for me," Denroy explained. "Certain scouts found your number for me and the location of your house."

Thomas Smith's jaw set. "From which I gather that you have had me watched! I strongly object to it!"

"Not exactly watched," Denroy corrected. "I wanted to be sure I didn't lose touch with you. We have such a lot in common—as you will see if we can have a discussion."

"Very well then," Thomas Smith sighed. "When shall I expect you?"

"I would much prefer that you came to me."

"That's impossible: I'm too busy. Since it is a matter of indifference to me whether we talk or not you will either have to come here, or drop the whole idea."

"There are various reasons why I cannot do that," Denroy temporized. "For my own part I would willingly do so, but there are three other affluent gentlemen whom I wish you to meet and they have certain equipment they wish you to see, which cannot be moved. So you must come to us."

"Very well, I'll make an exception. When shall I call?"

"Would this evening about eight be too much to ask?"

Thomas Smith glanced at his watch. "I'll be there. Where is your home?"

"The Larches, North Rise, Maida Vale. Easy to find."

Thomas Smith put the 'phone back on its cradle without further comment and stood thinking. Glenda came slowly forward and looked at him.

"I didn't hear the other side of the conversation, Torn," she said, "but I did gather enough to know that Denroy has got you to do as he wants—as he does with everybody. Why don't you stand out against him?"

"Chiefly because I want to find out exactly what he's after. He is one of those people who are a menace to the community, and the sooner I know how much of a menace the better. Since he won't come to me I must go to him."

"Just a moment!" Glenda caught at his arm. "Don't tell me you have one of those notions of yours that he needs rubbing out! He's very important. If you start eliminating him there'll be trouble."

"It doesn't concern me, Glenny, whether he's important or not. It is his ambitions in which I'm interested, and if they don't appear favorable towards everybody concerned I shall have to do something about it."

"When his 'phone call interrupted us you were going to tell me something—about yourself—"

"Yes, but it will have to wait. It's seven o'clock now and I have to be in Maida Vale by eight. You won't mind driving me over there?"

"Of course not, but I'm holding you to your promise to, finish your story about yourself at the earliest moment. In the meantime have I your permission to write an article about this house of yours?"

"By all means, but don't refer to the laboratory. That is private, as is also my admission that I am not entirely of this world."

"In any case I couldn't use that remark. It doesn't make sense You must be one thing or the other."

"Not necessarily, Glenny. The answer is really much simpler than you think—However, we must be on our way."

CHAPTER SIX
Unfit to live

During the swift journey back to London Glenda and Thomas Smith exchanged but little conversation. It was nearing eight when they reached North Rise, Maida Vale, and the residence of Alvin Denroy set well back from the street.

"Am I to wait for you?" Glenda asked, as Thomas Smith alighted from the car and looked about him.

"If you don't mind. I can't say how long I'll be but I certainly don't intend to delay matters."

"I suppose," Glenda said, through the open window, "it's silly for me to say that I'm afraid for you—but honestly I am! I'm sure Denroy has no good purpose in wanting to see you, and if anything should happen to you I—"

"Nothing will," Thomas Smith assured her, smiling. "I'm aware of the kind of man I'm dealing with. I'll handle him."

With that he turned, passed through the gateway of the residence, and went up the driveway. An immaculate butler admitted him and then conducted him to the library. Just inside it Thomas Smith paused and looked about him, his dark overcoat tightly buttoned. He had refused the manservant's offer to relieve him of his outdoor wear.

Alvin Denroy came forward with hand extended and a genial smile on his bulldog face. The other men had also risen and began acknowledgments and handshakes as Denroy made the introductions. Apparently each man was connected with an essential industry.

"My time is limited, gentlemen," Thomas Smith said briefly, settling down and shaking his head at the offer of cigars and drink.

"Of course," Denroy agreed, also sitting. "However, I have a proposition to put to you, Mister Smith, and I am confident that it will interest you."

Thomas Smith did not move a muscle. His magnetic eyes remained on Denroy's face—much to the latter's inner discomfiture.

"You have a number of strange gifts," Denroy proceeded. "You are a telepathist; you have the secret of making yourself invisible at will; you have the mastery of wealth and power. Yet apart from one or two unspectacular demonstrations of these powers you make little use of them. Why is that?"

"I thought," Thomas Smith replied, "you referred to a proposition, not a cross-examination."

"Sorry: I didn't mean to pry. What I mean is, you don't seem to realize the full extent of your genius."

"I know exactly what I can do, Mister Denroy, and if I didn't I could hardly picture you, or any of these gentlemen here being anxious to improve things for me."

"You are making it very difficult to conduct things in a friendly atmosphere!" one of the men protested.

"I didn't ask for this interview, did I? Come to the point, please!"

Denroy cleared his throat. "In return for assistance from you, Mister Smith, I am prepared to show you how best to obtain the complete mastery of the world! We realize of course that you are somebody different—a queer, dominant personality who has come amongst us from a source we do not know, but that is beside the point. We are not interested in your origin, only in what you can do."

"For your benefit," Thomas Smith added dryly.

"I didn't say that!" Denroy snapped.

"You thought it, though." Thomas Smith looked from one to the other. "Perhaps it would save time if I outlined your proposition for you? You want me to pry into the secrets of every leader in the world and give you information as to what is being planned. You want me to become the greatest Paul Pry in history, so you can enrich yourselves over and above the immense fortunes you have already accrued. In return for that you are prepared to steer me into a position of so-called dominance.

"Having gained that point you would eliminate me, which would leave you all in a position of supreme authority, able to wage destruction or beneficence at will, and as far as I can detect beneficence is foreign to you. I know everything you are up to, gentlemen, and in any case the price is not good enough. I don't want the mastery of the world."

Denroy stared. "You don't want it?"

"No. Which you, of course, find hard to understand."

"Then why are you amongst us if that isn't your aim?"

"Why I am amongst you is my own business. One thing I do perceive, and that is that you gentlemen are a definite menace to the community as a whole. I can go where I wish and read thoughts as I choose—and I do not like what I read in the thoughts of you men here. You have schemes that could bring the human race to destruction.

"You have the impudence to think that you could drag me into this, that you could precipitate things by having me learn from various leaders just what they plan. You have also talked over the idea of eliminating me if I should prove awkward. In the laboratory adjoining this library there is a lethal chamber in which you think you might dispose of me because I know too much about you."

All save Denroy were staring at Thomas Smith, stunned by the manner in which he had read their innermost thoughts. Not so Denroy. Though he showed no outward sign of his fury his fingers clenched tightly about the large glass paperweight on the desk beside him. Suddenly he threw it, with such violence and deadly aim that Thomas Smith had no chance to save himself. Stunned, he slumped out of his chair onto the floor.

"That wasn't very smart!" one of the men snapped, leaping up.

"No other way," Denroy told him. "I completely underestimated this fellow. We've got to be rid of him before he starts telling everybody how much he knows about us. Give me a hand to get him into the lab."

"You're not going to—" the aircraft man looked alarmed.

"I am going to kill him," Denroy stated deliberately. "I have a regard for my neck if you haven't for yours. Stop talking and help me."

Since there seemed to be nothing else for it Thomas Smith was picked up and carried across the room to a doorway. Denroy opened it and stepped into a small laboratory, the light switching itself on automatically as the door opened. Thomas Smith's dead weight was hauled across the space to a steel door and then set down for a moment.

Pulling the clamps away from the door Denroy swung it wide and went beyond. He inspected several cylinders, checked their tube connections to a switchboard in the laboratory, then gave a nod.

"Bring him in," he ordered—and Thomas Smith was dragged inside and dumped in the center of the metal floor. Denroy looked down at him for a moment, then stepped outside and clamped the door shut again.

"Nothing else for it," he decided. "We can't afford to let a man like that go running loose now we've been fool enough to let him read our minds. He's a menace!"

"Whose idea was it to bring him here anyway?" the oil man demanded. "I told you this would happen! We'll never get away with wiping him out, either. He's too celebrated a figure for the thing to pass off lightly!"

"Listen, there's one thing you're forgetting," Denroy said, breathing hard. "He came from nowhere in the first place, didn't he? If he utterly disappears, as mysteriously as he arrived, who's to know the difference? If he told anybody he was coming here we can always say he vanished from the midst of us . . . The fact remains he has to be eliminated and I remain sanguine that my recently-discovered war-gas will do it!"

Turning, he spun the knobs on the switch-panel, which controlled the outflow of gas from the cylinders within the lethal chamber. For five minutes he left them on at full pressure and then stood looking at the grim-faced men around him.

"He'll be dead, that's certain," one of the men said finally, "but that doesn't rid us of his body—or had you thought of that?"

"Certainly I have," Denroy snapped. "It's the most important thing of all, and here is the answer."

He nodded towards the further wall where there stood four large flasks filled with an ice-blue fluid, each flask tightly stoppered.

"Liquid air?" asked the transport man.

"Exactly. Used a lot in my business and will consume steel and turn it into dust, so it will certainly destroy flesh and bone. I think we can be rid of the corpse completely by destroying it with liquid air." Denroy looked at his watch, then at a switch on the panel.

"That opens the ventilator and allows the gas to disperse," he explained. "We'll give it fifteen minutes. Until then let's get back to the library. I need a drink."

The men followed each other out and had hardly got their drinks poured before there was a tap on the door and the butler appeared.

"Well?" Denroy asked him shortly. "I thought I told you we were not to be disturbed?"

"There's a Miss Carlyle, sir," the butler said. "From the *Clarion*. She would like a word with you."

"Ask her to come again: I can't be bothered now. Mister Smith is examining some equipment in the laboratory and we are awaiting his opinion. It's no time to—"

"Sorry," Glenda apologized, as she appeared pushing past the startled butler. "I could hear you from the hall and I don't like being kept waiting."

The butler started to protest, but Denroy dismissed him; then he studied Glenda.

"Well, Miss Carlyle?" he asked.

"I'm looking for Mister Smith," Glenda explained, coming forward and glancing about her. "Where is he? I notice his hat is here. I got rather weary of waiting in the car for him, especially as he told me he wouldn't be long."

"You mean you came with him?"

"Yes; I drove him here."

The men exchanged glances, then Denroy said: "Have a seat, Miss Carlyle. Mister Smith won't be very long. He's in the laboratory checking over some equipment."

"Oh—" Glenda settled herself, her expression half puzzled as her eyes strayed to the door towards which Denroy had glanced. Then she found him before her with a glass of wine in his hand. She took it and nodded her thanks.

"It is possible," Denroy said, "that our little conference with Mister Smith may last for quite a time even after he has finished checking the equipment. I think you would find it tiresome waiting. I'll give him a message for you if you like."

"I don't like," Glenda said, and took a sip of the wine as she watched Denroy's face intently.

"Is this visit supposed to be on behalf of the *Clarion*, or what?" the aircraft man snapped.

"I'm here simply because I am Mister Smith's 'Girl Friday'," Glenda answered. "Where he goes, I go. He asked me to wait for him, and I intend to."

Denroy cast a sidelong look at his colleagues; then Glenda, got to her feet decisively.

"With your permission?" she asked, and went to the laboratory door.

Denroy did not stop her. He watched her open the door and then go into the laboratory beyond.

"What's the idea, Al?" the aircraft man asked Denroy. "She'll be bound to discover he isn't there! She's dangerous! I thought you said nobody knew Smith had come here?"

"I guessed wrong, that's all," Denroy answered. "And it simply means we have one more person to be rid of, that's all. Follow me," he instructed, and with his friends behind him Denroy walked into the laboratory and closed the door.

Glenda looked up from glancing about her. Her expression showed that she had already guessed half of the truth.

"Where is he?" she demanded. "I thought you said he was in here?"

"He is," Denroy answered, then to his colleagues: "Grab her, boys!"

Before Glenda could save herself her arms and shoulders were seized and she was forced down into a chair and held there. She sat watching intently as Denroy gave her a malicious smile and then released the clamps on the door of the lethal chamber. The door swung slowly on its massive hinges as he pulled at it. Cautiously he sniffed the air within the chamber, nodded, and then stepped inside. In a moment or two he had dragged forth Thomas Smith's body and laid it in a corner.

"What have you done to him?" Glenda shouted, frantically fighting uselessly to free herself. "You've killed him!"

"In with her, boys," Denroy ordered. "Pity to have to do this but we can't be safe any other way."

Kicking and struggling Glenda was dragged across the floor to the chamber. She was almost within it when Thomas Smith spoke. His voice was cold and deliberate.

"Release Miss Carlyle, gentlemen, and turn to face me."

The four men hesitated, awe-stricken. They had their backs to Thomas Smith. Each man had been convinced that he was dead. It seemed impossible that a man could be steeped in poison gas for fifteen minutes and live. Slowly Glenda was released.

"Release that girl, gentlemen, and turn to face me!" Thomas Smith commanded, and was obeyed.

He was on his feet now. Glenda half started to speak in relief but he silenced her with a gesture. She stood watching him, and for the first time since she had known him she beheld the most unbelievable expression coming to his face. She realized that this must have been the look that Henry Armstrong and the tramp had seen and which, later, had sent them to their deaths.

It terrified her even though it had no appreciable effect upon her. On the four men just in front of her, however, the effect seemed akin to paralysis. They were motionless, not a finger moving, gazing at Thomas Smith with hypnotized intensity.

His eyes seemed to distend in the most extraordinary way until it was impossible for Glenda or the men to look anywhere else but at them. His voice seemed to come from far off.

"Normally, of course, your recently-invented war-gas would kill, but it happens that you are not dealing with a normal man. I have a mind far stronger than my body and since the body can only obey the mind I stayed alive—unhurt—the moment I recovered from the momentary unconsciousness produced by that blow you dealt me. I was quite conscious when you dragged me into that chamber, Denroy, but I waited to see what you did. Now I realize that not only my death but Miss Carlyle's as well was intended."

The eyes seemed bigger than ever. They had become enormous black orbs from the top of the cheekbones to the tip of the eyebrows. There was no demarcation between iris and pupil. It was like gazing into two gleaming black pools in the depths of which glowed green, lambent fire. In those terrible orbs, the face now seeming small by comparison, Glenda read an ageless wisdom and terrifying mental power. A sense of destruction and death hovered around her.

"Earlier in our conversation, gentlemen, I concluded that you were unfit to live because of the plans you have made," Thomas Smith continued. "What has happened since has not caused me to amend my opinion. I have plans, also."

There was silence for a moment and Glenda forced herself to look away from the glaring, alien eyes as she vaguely sensed the battering of a stupendous mental force. It was only when Thomas Smith spoke to her directly, his voice as quiet as it had always been, that she turned. He was standing beside her, looking down on her with that half amused smile. His eyes, his expression, were normal again.

"Did—did I dream all that a moment ago?" she asked. "About you, I mean. Did you really look so terrifying?"

"It was not a dream, Glenny, and I think we had better leave here."

She nodded quickly and looked at the four men as she passed them. They were standing motionless, like figures in a waxworks.

"Are they dead?" she questioned, as Thomas Smith urged her across the laboratory.

"Not yet. They have post-hypnotic orders to obey."

Glenda wondered vaguely what the orders could be, but Thomas Smith was evidently in no mood to elaborate. He led her through the library and out into the hall. The butler hovered, surprised at their departure without his having been informed of it beforehand.

"Good night, madam—sir," he said gravely.

"You will find Mister Denroy and his friends in the laboratory," Thomas Smith said. "You'd better see if they need you."

"Yes, sir." The butler looked mystified. "Very good."

The moment he had seen Thomas Smith and Glenda out he went to the laboratory and opened the door, looking in on the four men moving about within. They seemed to be preoccupied in studying the huge stoppered flasks by the wall.

"Mr. Smith suggested, sir, that you might need me," the manservant remarked.

He was ignored. The men still surveyed the flasks and then began to move them. Vaguely offended, the butler withdrew and closed the laboratory door.

Once in the car Glenda looked at Thomas Smith sharply as she switched on the ignition.

"Why did you tell the manservant to go and see if Denroy wanted anything?" she asked.

"To prove, Glenry, that those four men are still alive after we have gone. Before very long all of them will be dead, but the way it has been arranged the butler can vouch for it that I am not responsible, since we shall be some distance off when the men die. All right, Glenny, drive on—back to my home."

"I've my editor to think of before that," she protested. "He has never seen anything of me since I set off to court this morning. I'd better put in an appearance."

"As you wish," Thomas Smith conceded, and relaxed.

As she drove through the London streets, Thomas Smith quiet beside her, Glenda kept seeing again that extraordinary being who had stood in the laboratory—that metamorphosed Thomas Smith who had become something so terrifying that she had been forced to turn away from looking at him. She asked herself why she was now seated so casually beside him, driving him along because he had asked her to. Bt rights she should have been getting as far away from him as possible, convinced as she was at last of his nonhuman origin.

"And yet you don't," Thomas Smith remarked.

"No," she admitted absently, and then gave a start as she realized he had read her thoughts.

"You stay beside me, Glenny, because you are loyal," he said. "Because you love me. That's something I shall always remember. Please don't let that business in the laboratory upset you. It's over and finished with. I would rather you had not seen my expression, but it couldn't be helped. At other times I have turned my back to you to save you the experience."

"Did you look at my mother like that when you cured her?" Glenda muttered, threading amidst the traffic.

"Good heavens, no. Only anger makes me look like that!"

"The face contorts, yes, but it doesn't make one's eyes go twice as large until they look like—like I just don't know what," Glenda finished helplessly. "If ever I became sure of your not belonging to the human race it was in that laboratory tonight."

"But I do belong to the human race!" he protested.

"I don't believe it, Tom. I couldn't, after that! No human being ever looked like you did."

"I still insist that I am a human being."

"How can you be when you've as good as admitted you don't belong to this world?"

"I said—not entirely."

"And what kind of an answer is that?" Glenda demanded. "Why can't you tell me the truth?"

"Because I don't think you'd believe it, and because I have orders not to do so."

Glenda drove on in silence for a time, then when she was on a clear stretch of main road leading into the heart of the city she spoke again.

"I have a theory about you," she said. "You are from another planet. I don't know which—maybe Mars, Venus, or somewhere. I'm not well up in astronomy, but I have read some imaginative fiction. Probably you're from Mars, since some writers say that it has an older civilization than ours—hidden below the surface—and therefore the people on it are must be far cleverer than we are. Now it is also possible that some of our early races were smart enough to know how to travel across space, and perhaps they escaped from the Deluge and other disasters and later settled on

Mars. That would mean that if you are from Mars you are partly from Earth, too, since your ancestors started from here way back in the dim beginning of history."

"Interesting," Thomas Smith commented, musing.

"Add to that the meteors seen just before you appeared, and the chunks of iron with rivets in them which I saw myself—that could suggest a space machine, and with you inside it. You survived the crash and came amongst us. That laboratory annex in your home contains radio equipment for getting in touch with your home planet. Your home is probably Mars—the 'home' referred to on that scratch pad of yours in the lab."

Thomas Smith laughed. "You've worked out quite an admirable theory, Glenny, and I congratulate you upon it. Only it is quite wrong. I am not from Mars or Venus."

"Well—the stars, then!" Glenda suggested. "Some other planet, anyway."

"No. I am of this world, my dear. Earlier I was going to waive instructions and tell you all about it. Now I see what an inventive mind you have got I think I'll let you guess the answer. If you haven't done so by the time I am due to depart, I'll tell you all about it."

"But, Tom, if you are not from another world there is no barrier to us marrying."

"There is, Glenny, and a very real one! You'll see why in time."

Glenda gave it up, at least for the moment. Thomas Smith's inscrutable smile, that look as if he were enjoying the prank of a child, nettled her somewhat but she managed to keep her temper. In any case she had no chance to argue further about the matter for the *Clarion* offices had been reached.

"I've got to explain being away all day," Glenda said worriedly. "I haven't much to hand in the way of information, either. Unless I write up something about your new home."

Thomas Smith roused himself from thought. "I'll come with you, Glenny. Probably I can deal with your editor."

"More than likely!"

Glenda found his hand at her elbow and they entered the great building together. As they went along the brilliantly-lighted entrance hall Thomas Smith asked a question.

"You haven't yet met a man by the name of Gregory Vane, have you?"

Glenda thought for a moment and then shook her head. "Not that I can recall. Why?"

"You will. Probably in the next few minutes. "

This time her bewilderment was complete. Thomas Smith could not possibly have read this fact from her mind because the name meant nothing to her; yet he seemed to be sure enough that such a man would shortly come into her life. Nearly too confused to think straight she entered the lift with Thomas Smith beside her and they were taken to the fourth floor and the news editor's office.

He was not alone. A youngish, good-looking man with thick dark hair and intellectual features was deep in conversation with him—but he broke it off and rose as the two of them entered.

"Sorry to interrupt, chief," Glenda apologized. "I'll come in again later—"

"Stay right here," the news editor told her. "You too, Mister Smith. I want you both to meet Mister Gregory Vane."

"Glad to know you," Gregory Vane said, apparently not noticing Glenda's fascinated stare and Thomas Smith's inscrutable smile. "In fact you, Mr. Smith, are the very man I want to talk to!"

"Indeed, Mr. Vane? Upon which subject?"

"You! I'm a scientist and I have a few theories about you I'd like to discuss with you."

"I'm afraid I have little information to offer you, Mr. Vane."

"Oh, come now!" The good-looking young man's eyes were bright with challenge. "The miracle man in person and he has nothing to offer! I think that you have so much to offer that you can virtually stand science on its ear! I was just asking the news editor here how I might get in touch with you when in you walked!"

"As for you, Glenny, what do you mean by walking out on me?" the news editor demanded. "What are you paid for? Not to keep constant company with Mr. Smith, I can assure you!"

"You gave me the exclusive job of writing up about him," Glenda pointed out. "So I have to be with him quite a lot. I'll have a column of today's activities in before the paper goes to press."

"You'd better! You— 'scuse me!" The news editor picked up the telephone. He listened and his gaze became fixed. "Yes, yes, go on," he said abruptly, making notes on his scratch pad. "All four of them, you say?" He whistled and then rang off.

"Something big?" Glenda asked.

"I'll say! Four of the biggest commercial giants in the country have just made a suicide pact and killed themselves off together by jumping into a bath of liquid air! I just got the tip-off from Griffiths of the Yard. He keeps me posted on things like that when he has permission to tell the Press. The police are having a look to see if there is any evidence of foul play. You happen to know anything about this, Mister Smith?"

"Even if I do, no good purpose could be served by my admitting it," he answered. Then he dismissed the subject entirely and said: "I am here chiefly to make excuses for Miss Carlyle. She has been out with me ever since the court acquitted me this morning and I believe she has quite an interesting story to tell of our wanderings."

"I have everything except what I want," Glenda sighed. "I don't know where Mister Smith hails from, and he won't tell me. All he will say is—the answer's simpler than you think."

"Glad to hear something is," the news editor growled. "For myself, I'm completely baffled by you, Mister Smith, but I don't hold it against you. Strictly off the record, I think you're doing a good job amongst us, though I don't know what you're aiming at."

"I'm leaving town for a while on business," Thomas Smith remarked.

"You are?" Glenda looked surprised. "You've never mentioned it before."

"An oversight, Glenny. I have some special work to do. The moment I'm back in town I'll get in touch with you."

"Then you're leaving that wonderful home of yours just after you've got it all fixed up?" Glenda asked.

"Only for a while. I know you are wondering if it is safe to leave it with so much valuable equipment inside it. It is quite safe—rest assured on that. I have it protected by an electrical barrier and there is nobody with sufficient intelligence to break the barrier down."

The news editor looked at Glenda and she looked back at him. Gregory Vane, however, was studying Thomas Smith intently.

"Practically everybody accepts your statements, Mister Smith," he said. "Miss Carlyle and the editor, for instance, but I'm afraid I don't. I suggest you make the statements you do because you have foreknowledge of everything that is going to happen. You know already that your home will not be touched in your absence."

Thomas Smith smiled. "You are a man of considerable intelligence—and curiosity, Mister Vane."

"I think for myself, that's all—and being a scientist helps a lot. That's why I want to talk to you, if I may, before you leave on this trip of yours."

"I'm afraid the time does not permit," Thomas Smith said, and turned to shake Glenda's hand in farewell.

"Mister Smith, I know your secret," Gregory Vane said quietly. "I could tell it to the world right now and everybody would probably say I'm crazy, yet it would be the truth. It is so surprisingly logical, too. Maybe other scientists have guessed it, but have not come into the open as I have."

Thomas Smith faced him. "May I ask why you have, Mister Vane? What good do you hope to achieve by telling your theory to the world?"

"It isn't a theory: it's fact, and my reason for wanting to publish it is that it could do my career a lot of good."

"How so?"

"In the same way that Lister's discovery of antiseptic made him immortal. It would cause me to become the discoverer of a new science, and the first in the field gets the credit. You cannot blame me for wanting to better my lot as a research scientist."

"You mean for personal gain you would give me away?"

Vane's eyes gleamed. "Then you admit I'm right!"

"Since I know what you are thinking I cannot do anything else. However, I also perceive that you have the instincts of a man who would respect my confidence if I asked for it."

"Certainly."

The news editor's head was jerking back and forth from one man to the other as though it were on wires. Glenda was looking perplexed, trying to salve something tangible from the conversation, and failing utterly.

"I have it in my power," Thomas Smith said, "to make you completely forget the theory you have formed about me, but, satisfied that you are a man of honor, I leave you in possession. I ask that you keep it to yourself until I say you may expound it. When that time comes I will also give you written and other corroborative evidence in support."

"You have my word," Vane said promptly, shaking hands. "This is the most wonderful thing that ever happened—not only to me as a scientist, but to the whole world."

On that the subject dropped and left the news editor seething.

"Will one of you fellows tell me what in hell goes on between, you? If there's a story, I want it!"

"You will have it finally," Thomas Smith assured him. "Miss Carlyle will write it up for you. I'll see to that. In the meantime I have things to do. Good-bye for now, Glenny—and to you, Mister Vane."

Thomas Smith departed, and the news editor compressed his lips. "A great help you are, Mister Vane! You know as much as Smith, apparently, and won't say a thing!"

"You wouldn't expect me to break my word to him, would you?"

"No, I suppose not. It's galling, though. I suppose you couldn't hint at anything?"

"I could," Gregory Vane smiled, "but I'm not going to. I suggest you just keep on guessing." He glanced at his watch. "Well, I must be going. Now I've seen Mister Smith I'm satisfied—"

"Can you wait another ten minutes?" Glenda broke in quickly.

"I can, yes, but why?"

"I'd like a chat with you, Mister Vane." Glenda gave him a frank look. "First, though, I've a story to dash off on my day with Mister Smith; then I'll be free."

"Okay. I'll wait."

* * *

Whilst Thomas Smith was returning home by a late local train, Chief-Inspector Brough was in his office at Scotland Yard. He was in the worst of tempers and Detective-Sergeant Cavendish in his own corner knew better than to interrupt his superior's obviously disquieting thoughts.

Finally Brough shrugged his broad shoulders in a manner that seemed to suggest he was resigned to the inevitable.

"Suicide it will have to be," he said, "even though we know that isn't the right answer."

"I should think it isn't!" Cavendish protested. "I've never heard of anything so fantastic as four millionaires, with everything in the world they can wish for, leaping into a bath of liquid air and putting an end to themselves. Thoroughly, too! Nothing but the charred remains of their bodies and a few identifying marks where the liquid air had not reached. I don't think I ever saw anything quite so horrible as that scene in the laboratory."

"Nevertheless we can't prove foul play," Brough said. "I've been thinking it out and there's nothing we can pin on Thomas Smith."

"There ought to be something," Cavendish insisted. "We know that he and Glenda Carlyle were almost the last people to see the four men alive, and—"

"Yes—almost!" Brough interrupted. "That's what trips us up! The butler told us he saw the four men alive after Thomas Smith had left with Miss Carlyle and that very fact prevents us making a charge. The butler swears that Thomas Smith did not return to the residence, so suicide it will have to be. Knowing Smith as we do, we can be pretty sure that he did some of his hypnosis and forced those four men to kill themselves."

"Well since Smith is known to be a man of peculiar mental powers haven't we enough to go on in that fact alone to arrest him on suspicion? I tell you sir, the man's a menace! He just blots out everybody he doesn't like! How much longer is the public going to stand by and watch us do exactly nothing?"

"I know just what everybody will say, same as you do," Brough growled, "but in this instance we are hamstrung. If I arrested Smith, granting I could ever get my hands on him, the main point against me would be that he had left the house when the men killed themselves. If I tried to prove hypnosis as the cause of the men killing themselves I'd not get anywhere."

"Why shouldn't you?"

"Because Thomas Smith would bring in mental experts to testify that nobody can be hypnotized to do anything injurious to themselves, the reason being that the law of self preservation is the dominant instinct of the human mind—and so on those grounds I'd never be able to prove to a jury that Smith had hypnotized not one, but four strong minded men to kill themselves. I personally am convinced that he did, but I could never prove it definitely."

"You mean," the Sergeant hazarded, "that Smith is able to make people kill themselves if he wishes it?"

"Exactly! Our experts have based their conclusions on the fact that nobody has ever yet been amongst us with the terrific mental power of Thomas Smith. No," Brough sighed, "there's nothing we can do, Cavendish. Even if it costs us our jobs in the finish, I much prefer to leave that fellow alone. He's the biggest enigma we've ever come up against."

Brough said no more. As far as he was concerned, the case of the four magnates was one of suicide—and while he arrived at this decision Glenda was seated in her car half a mile from the city garage where she intended to park, with Gregory Vane at her side. It seemed an extraordinary change to her to have a young, vital, and entirely understandable man beside her. It did much to break the extraordinary spell that Thomas Smith held over her.

"Very kind of you to give me a lift this far, Miss Carlyle," Gregory Vane said. "It'll save me fifteen minutes getting home."

"At this hour that will be a help," Glenda smiled. "It's nearly midnight—or perhaps your wife is accustomed to you knocking about at all hours?"

"Wife? I'm not married. I live in rooms and spend as little time as possible in them. Every waking moment I am in the laboratories, either doing routine work or making experiments of my own. With all the equipment around me and time on my hands I might as well."

"Yes, just as well," Glenda agreed, satisfied that she had discovered he was unmarried.

He said: "This is a marvelous car you've got! I never saw one quite like it before. If this is what the *Clarion* provide for its staff I must be in the wrong business!"

"Mr. Smith bought this car for me for services rendered—as a guide, I mean."

"Nothing cheap or ordinary for Mister Smith!"

"If only I knew as much about him and his origin as you do, Mister Vane, I'd be a much happier woman," Glenda sighed.

"Why are you so interested in his origin?"

"Apart from common curiosity, Mister Vane, I want to find out why there is such a barrier to my marrying him. I'm willing and so is he—but he insists that we can't. I suppose you know why not?"

"Yes." Gregory Vane looked pensive. "Yes, I do—but I didn't know things were that serious between you. Certainly you can never marry each other, Miss Carlyle, so forget all about it." He got out of the car. "Thanks for everything. Be seeing you again one of these days, I expect."

"I can always be found at the *Clarion* offices in the late evening," she answered, and with that he nodded, and then closed the car door.

Thoughtfully, Glenda started up the engine and then swung the great car into the side street that led to the garage. She liked Gregory Vane quite a lot, she decided. Since Thomas Smith was, for some mystic reason, forever beyond her reach, perhaps she might do worse than cultivate the young, sincere scientist. At least he behaved like a human being.

CHAPTER SEVEN
Revelations

When Thomas Smith left the *Clarion* offices he apparently stepped into the unknown. Nobody, it seemed saw him leave the building and he did not return to his home. In some ways this was perhaps a blessing for him for all manner of people, from so-called expert telepathists; people with incurable diseases, all wanting their own selfish demands satisfied, had assembled outside his residence.

Glenda was puzzled by Thomas Smith's disappearance, but to her surprise—and relief—it was nothing like the hurt she had expected to experience to lose him. For one thing she had Gregory Vane in mind. With Thomas Smith's continued absence, day after day and no report from him, Glenda even found herself wondering how she had ever become so attached to him.

Then, by degrees, from various sources throughout the world, there came into the offices of the *Clarion* and other newspapers items that suggested the strange power of Thomas Smith was at work. First there came from Vienna the intimation that Dr. Franz Yaheff, the noted specialist, had discovered an instantaneous cure for cancer.

This in itself was epoch-making—in the medical world at least—and in its incipiency warranted headlines; until it was supplanted by the news that Boyd Irwen, the great American oculist, had at last discovered how to make an artificial eye. Tests he had made had shown that the blind could see perfectly with it.

These two discoveries, marking an enormous stride toward the greater comfort of the human race, tended to overshadow other scraps of information wherein it appeared that totally independent workers, sometimes separated by thousands of miles had happened up on the formulae for curing all manner of minor ailments. Each man and woman responsible for these great ideas declared that they had just 'thought of them', but both Gregory Vane and Glenda were inclined to wonder if the information had not been somehow willed into their minds by the beneficence and mysterious power of Thomas Smith. Glenda in particular could not help but remember how closely Thomas Smith had questioned her as to which were the prevalent incurable ills of the time.

She half expected, after hearing of these discoveries that Thomas Smith would return to London, but there was still no sign of him. Instead there was a cessation of medical discoveries, and instead engineers and scientists seemed to develop their own 'brainwaves'.

New and safe uses for atomic power were announced, and the by-products were used to the fullest cheapest advantage. Ideas were put forth which made commercial interplanetary travel a certainty within a few years, and most extraordinary thing of all, nations gradually ceased to revile each other.

When this newest development in daily affairs occurred, Thomas Smith had been absent for a fortnight. In fact his advent had almost been forgotten in the succession of unexpected announcements. Glenda, still true to her memory of him, and wondering if he would ever come back, suggested as nearly as she dared that it was his influence alone which was responsible for the change in the affairs of men. Without the definite facts at her command, however, she found it difficult to write convincingly. Her articles on Thomas Smith she reserved for her personal remembrances of him, putting into her work every facet of his composite character.

The only person with whom she could exchange views was Gregory Vane, and it pleased her that he had sought her of his own volition. In a fortnight from their first meeting their friendship had become firmly cemented. He made it a habit to meet her each evening as she left the *Clarion* office, a time that he said coincided with his own time of departure from the research laboratory.

"Suppose," Glenda said one evening, as she sat with him in a supper-bar, "that Tom never returns? Doesn't that release you from your promise not to tell what you know about him?"

"I don't think so, Glenny," Gregory Vane replied, musing. "I gave him my word to keep quiet until he gives me permission to speak. If he never gives permission I shall never speak. That's all there is to it."

"Why the necessity for silence? What difference can it make?"

"As far as I can see it would have completely upset his plans for world-betterment if his secret had become known—for the simple reason that he would have been so besieged by scientists and curiosity-mongers he would hardly have been able to turn round. Had the truth got out he might even have been put in an asylum."

"With his powers he could have got out easily enough."

"Very probably, but it is much simpler for him not to have the need, isn't it?"

"Much," agreed a man who had settled at the next table.

Glenda and Gregory Vane both turned sharply. Together they absorbed the details of the dark coat and hat and the white features.

"Tom!" Glenda breathed in amazement. "It's you, isn't it?"

"Yes, Glenny. Sorry if I startled you." Then when Glenda and Gregory Vane had moved to his table Thomas Smith added: I got back to London late this evening and rang up the *Clarion* office. They told me you had left. I didn't give my name. I'm not anxious to have people chasing me for information."

He paused for a moment and ordered a meal as the waiter came over. The man went away again, entirely unaware of his customer's identity.

"You have been behind these recent discoveries, haven't you?" Gregory Vane asked, his voice low. "And also the change in world thought towards a more settled state of things?"

"Yes, I have. It seemed to me that in the political field, at least, humanity had too much science and not enough sense, so I've altered things to make the future safe. There won't be any war, you know," he finished.

"If you say so, there won't," Gregory Vane agreed.

"There's no certainty of it," Glenda objected.

"There is when I say there won't be," Thomas Smith assured her—and he said it with conviction not egotism. "As to the change of heart in political outlook, the sudden friendliness instead of hostility, the answer is simple. During my world tour I put into the mind of each country's leader a full awareness of what his biggest enemy is planning. You perceive the outcome? The leader of every country has to be pleasant because he isn't sure how much the other fellow knows about him! It makes war impossible. Nobody can fight a war when his innermost plans are known to the enemy, any more than you can play any kind of game when your intended moves are known to your opponent... As to the stockpiles of atomic weapons, which play such a big part on the political chessboard, I think it will be found that they will never be needed. This change of heart throughout every country will end in the bombs and other weapons being broken down for their by-product usefulness."

Glenda stared, her mouth slightly open. Gregory Vane looked at her and chuckled to himself.

"All right, laugh!" she exclaimed. "I've never yet been able to get over the fact that Tom here predicts things with absolute certainty, even to my meeting you."

"You are going to be married soon, of course?" Thomas Smith asked.

"We—we haven't thought of it yet," Gregory Vane protested, embarrassed.

"You will. On a sunny morning in July this year, the twelfth to be exact, you'll both leave Saint Peter's church as man and wife, and on that day, Glenny, you will know for the first time why you and I could never marry."

"And I don't find out until then?" she demanded.

"I shall make it my wedding present to you. The one mystery you have never been able to solve, and which is so simple when you know it. However, to get back to cases. I think my touring is now over, that I have done all I need. I came to tell you both that I am leaving."

"For good?" Glenda's voice dropped. "But you can't, Tom! You're doing such wonderful things in the world!"

"There is no more to do," he answered simply. "I have set humanity on the right track by giving it the correct ideas, or at least I have put those ideas into the minds best fitted to receive them—and there my work ends."

"Your work?" Glenda repeated. "You mean that was your reason for coming here? To put the human race to rights?"

"Partly. That is insofar that what human beings do today will pattern posterity." Thomas Smith paused for a moment and then to Glenda he added: "All this was pre-destined, Glenny. It had to happen."

"I'm still baffled, Tom."

"The best thing we can do is go to my home, he said. " I have no wish to delay things any longer before departing, but I did promise you a story. It needs my laboratory to do it properly. It is not far from midnight, but perhaps you can both spare the time?"

"Try and stop us!" Glenda exclaimed, getting quickly to her feet. "I can have the car out of the garage in five minutes—and we'll be on our way."

And they were. In half-an-hour the car had brought them to Thomas Smith's residence. Mid-way up the drive however he told Glenda to stop.

"You can't get through the electrical barrier," he explained. "I can because I'm impervious to it. I'll go ahead and switch off the current. Don't move until I come back."

He had returned in five minutes and the run up the driveway was completed. Once in the house he led the way to the laboratory, suggesting refreshment first but finding the offer refused since Glenda and Gregory Vane had already had a meal.

"This is certainly some lab you have here," Gregory Vane declared, gazing about him. "Looks like the nerve-center of a high-powered radio or TV station."

"It isn't though," Thomas Smith smiled. "Agreed everything is electrical, but it has nothing to do with radio or television. Nor is the lab powered from the ordinary main. I use an atomic power-pack which you can hear humming behind that protective door there."

Glenda glanced towards the door and nodded. She had already been aware of that droning when she had first stumbled into this queer, complicated place.

"It would perhaps save a lot of explanation if you took a look at this," Thomas Smith said, and crossing to a cabinet brought out a file. From it he took a much-creased and faded newspaper and handed it over.

"As a newspaper woman, Glenny, this edition of the *World Times* will interest you," he said.

"*World Times?*" Glenda frowned as she unfolded the paper. "I've never heard of it—" She broke off with a start, gazing at extraordinary headlines:

MUZEEUM REKORDS DESTROID
HISTRY SEKSHUN GUTTED

"What on earth does this mean?" she asked blankly. "It looks like the effort of a school-kid! What museum? What history section?"

Thomas Smith smiled. "That, Glenny, is a reputable daily paper with the highest paid columnists, even if they do have numbers instead of names. Observe the date."

Glenda found it—**January 27, 2302.**

"This is ridiculous!" she protested. "It's dated nearly three-hundred years ahead of today."

"Just so, and yet the paper is old and faded. I had it in the files for several years before I dug it out at the last moment and brought it along with me as proof."

"Proof of what?"

"Proof of the fact that I belong not to the present day but to the year 2306, three centuries ahead. That is what I meant when I said I am not entirely of this world—'world' in that sense meaning the present era."

Glenda stared at the paper in fascination, examining the amazing advertisements and incredible spelling—then she realized the paper was not newsprint at all, but some very fine metallic substance. She looked up at last into Thomas Smith's amused features.

"Simply stated, I am out of 'Time'," he said. "Mister Vane here, being a scientist, had arrived at that conclusion, through his own analysis of my behavior. I have come for a definite reason. I came to restore the records lost in the museum fire."

Thomas Smith motioned to chairs and then continued: "You see, I live three centuries ahead of you, in a city which is the chief city of the world. It has the name of Monopolis, derived from the word 'Monopoly' and meaning it is the major controlling center. In my own time and space I am a scientific historian with the number of JN-476. Long ago names were replaced by numbers: In our time there is equality of the sexes, marriage by permission of the Eugenics Council, destruction of the dangerous and unfit, and so on; in my time many of the theories of today are established facts.

"Today a great deal of experimenting with telepathy is proceeding. In my time the experiments have achieved fruition into an accomplished art. Every man and woman can read thoughts as simply as speaking, and that in itself has destroyed all underhanded work, threat of war, criminal tendency, and so forth. When thoughts can be read the last barrier to secrecy has gone. Secrecy is the root cause of strife. One has to live aright, or perish."

Glenda opened her handbag and began taking notes.

"Some time ago—in my era—a scientist discovered how to travel back and forth through the centuries. You would not understand the intricacies, but I can tell you that it amounts to moving physically just as one does from side to side or up and down. Time being an abstract quantity it demands a mathematical machine to move you through it. Time is actually no more than a hypothetical river, different periods of time being akin to ships at different parts of the river—some near to the source, others to the mouth. The necessary machinery can drive a ship backward or forward along the river: so can the necessary mathematical equipment drive one back and forth along the time-stream.

"However, it was found that our history records of the earlier centuries had in part been destroyed by fire, so to complete them it was decided that a scientist must go back to the earlier time and gather the necessary data to full in the blanks. I was selected and traveled here. The machine I used could also fly in case I materialized over an ocean but through a fault in the mechanism it exploded on my arrival . . . Hence a meteorite shower, so-called, when I materialized over Sussex. Hence the rivets in the metal pieces."

"The pieces of metal then were the remains of your time-machine?" Glenda asked.

"Yes. My next move was to go to London. In some instances I knew exactly what to expect because not all the history records were destroyed, but in other cases I had to find my way. Hence my uncertainty at times and confidence at others."

There was quiet for a moment, then Thomas Smith proceeded: "The records showed that in this present year, because of the intervention of a stranger who called himself Thomas Smith, peace became established throughout the world and humanity took the first real step to emancipation. That proved that I must be Thomas Smith and that I would do exactly as the records showed. It was inevitable because it had already happened. My job was simply to make it come true, in which I could not possibly fail because the record had shown it to be so.

"There is no record, however, of my other experiences—such as my acquittal by the court, my friendship with you, Glenny, and other matters, but there is a reference to an explosion destroying Baynton Hall—tonight!"

Gregory Vane started. "Tonight?"

"Exactly." Thomas Smith laughed. "The explanation is simple. I intend tonight to return to my own Time and when I go I shall leave behind an atomic-detonator which will destroy this place and all traces of me. Time travel will not be discovered for a couple of centuries, and because history says it is so, so be it. I am repeating actions, which, to me, are in the past. To you, in the future."

"Very confusing," Glenda said, wrinkling her forehead. "Just the same, there are still things puzzling me. Those diamonds, Tom. Where did they come from?"

"I brought them with me along with several others. Records said that diamonds, in the past, were fabulously valuable. To us they are only carbon, uranium isotopes being the basis of our currency. I set out with a pocketful of diamonds knowing their value here, and a suit of clothes designed for the era in which I would need them."

"I see. How did you get involved with those various men and kill them?"

"In each case I read their thoughts from a distance and then intervened."

"Those rocks and stuff you picked up on our tour—why did you do that?"

"The grass, rock, and sea water I collected were specimens to take home for record purposes, as samples of a past time."

"Invisibility and your escape from the lethal chamber?" Glenda persisted.

"Both can be explained by the mastery of the body by the mind. Any material thing obeys the mind, if it is strong enough. By that process one can will oneself to be invisible; can will oneself to overcome death—can accomplish almost anything. Unfortunately death is not entirely conquered yet because we have not fully mastered the curse of age. As one grows older the mind becomes less able to keep control of the situation . . . That bowl of flowers I had your mother pick—I willed into them the thought of eternal life, and because mind is above matter they will never die."

"In the same way, I suppose, you created forgetfulness and so on in the men you met?"

"Yes. The minds of the people of today offer no barrier to a mind like mine, developed three centuries ahead of the present, with all the all the power and refinement that implies." There was a silence, then Thomas Smith resumed.

"Reverting to more personal matters, Glenny. I knew that you and Gregory Vane would meet for the very good reason that our records show you were married—or will be, from your present point of view—on the 12th of July this year. Eighteen months later a son will be born. That, too, is recorded."

Glenda gave Gregory Vane a glance and he stirred uneasily.

"In this age," Thomas Smith said, thinking, "the sexes are curiously diffident of each other. In mine they are equal and biological process is discussed openly. It explains why I, trained to the equality of man and woman, got so confused when I realized how firm a hold you had on me, Glenda. I might even have yielded to that hold—except for one glaring historical fact that made it impossible. As I told you, I intend to explain why we could never marry, and I am leaving a sealed message for you at my bank to be delivered to you on your wedding day. You will forgive the suspense?"

"I've no choice," Glenda answered. "Tell me something. Going back to invisibility. Why didn't you appear in a photograph?"

"You can deceive the eye, Glenny, but not the lens. The eye sees me here because it is aided by complementary mental senses like sound, sight, touch, and imagination. That lens of the camera has no such assistance. It registers purely what is in the light waves at that moment. It could not register me because by all normal law I am not yet born. In a word, the lens never lies, but the eyes do."

"Why," asked Gregory Vane, "didn't you reveal your secret? Was it because you believed it might hamper your activities?"

"Yes. It would have created such confusion that my mission might well have ended in failure. I had orders from my own time not to reveal my origin until my mission was finished: that is why I am talking now."

Glenda came to an end of making her notes. Her eyes were bright with excitement.

"There's never been a story like this!" she exclaimed. "Never! Granting anybody will ever believe it, that is."

"You have Gregory as a witness to what I have said—a scientist who can verify the finer details for those who are inclined to doubt—as, of course, some are bound to do. On the other hand you have this newspaper of three centuries hence, and you have these coins . . . "

Thomas Smith gave Glenda a handful of queerly designed bronze-looking medallions, stamped 'World Federation, 2306.'

He said: "They are made from a metal unknown in this age. The paper, too, is made of a by-product of the same metal. There is your proof . . . And that," he finished quietly, "is about all. My records are complete and I have all the materials I want for filling in the blanks in our files. My job as a roving historian is done. In this laboratory here you behold the equipment necessary for returning me to my own time. Since my original machine was destroyed I had had to build a new one, various engineering firms supplying different parts so no one firm knew the secret . . . And here is the machine itself."

He crossed the laboratory, moved a sliding door and pulled out an object on wheels, with two short wings jutting from the sides. It was made of polished metal with two small portholes. Glenda and Gregory looked at in fascination, then inside the airlock on a maze of complicated controls.

"I suppose," Glenda asked, "there's no chance of us coming with you for the greatest story of all time?"

"There isn't room, Glenny. I rather wish there were, but the idea of your coming too was something that never occurred to me when I made the machine."

"When did you make it?" Gregory Vane asked.

"During the first few days when I had taken over this place. That was why I wanted peace and quiet. However, neither of you can come with me, because history says distinctly that I—Thomas Smith—returned alone, That cannot be altered. If I ever return here, though, something may be done."

"Do you think—you ever will?" Glenda asked.

"I don't know, Glenny. I don't know . . . It has been wonderful knowing you," he continued, gripping her hand warmly. "And you have the right companion in Gregory here—that I know. And don't forget to be out of here within 10 minutes of my machine vanishing. The atomic detonator will go off then. Obviously you will get away safely otherwise you couldn't be married in July next!"

Glenda laughed uncomfortably over the paradox of the situation, and started to ask another question—but Thomas Smith did not give her the chance to finish it. He shook hands with Gregory and then climbed swiftly into the airlock of the machine.

The curious scientific equipment inside the contraption was sufficient to cause the electrical components of the laboratory to start functioning under remote control. Silent, awe-struck, Glenda and Gregory watched the fantastic display as the machine became hazed in amethyst light.

It shimmered, became so brilliant it was hard to gaze at it; then by degrees it became transparent and with a sudden swoosh of hot air was gone, the space was empty.

"Better get out," Gregory said quickly, and gripped Glenda's arm. Remember what he told us."

She nodded, and together they hurried from the laboratory. Glenda had hardly driven the car a safe distance along the road beyond the driveway before the entire mass of Baynton Hall appeared to lift clean out of the earth, blasted into fragments by an explosion of inconceivable power.

Miles away windows were broken by the blast. The car in which Glenda and Gregory sat rocked but did not overturn, the high bank acting as a baffle. Then Glenda began driving on again. On the way were crowds of inquisitive people heading into the night.

Glenda got her story into the *Clarion* offices at 1.30 in the morning, and the news editor, who had departed for the night, was called back to print a special edition for the strangest tale ever turned in. He did not say whether he believed it or not—but he printed it. The coins and newspaper from 2306, together with the other queer mysteries always attached to Thomas Smith, were evidently enough to convince him.

Next day the world knew the story—and the only man who could explain it so that it made sense was Gregory Vane. His lectures on Thomas Smith made him famous. Glenda's articles on Thomas Smith, and her recent biography of him, raised her to an envious literary pinnacle.

*   *   *

As Thomas Smith had predicted, July 12th was a sunny day, and though the wedding was exciting, Glenda was even more excited by the arrival of a small parcel, given to her by a solicitor's clerk as she was leaving St. Peter's church. Not until the celebration was over, and she and Gregory were on the train for the first lap of their honeymoon did she open the package Thomas Smith had left for her.

She found herself looking at a diamond of such size and luster it stunned her. It exceeded those she had already seen in Thomas Smith's possession.

Then she unfolded the letter Thomas Smith had written. She read it slowly, with Gregory reading it over her shoulder. It ran:

"My dear Glenny,

"For the many kindnesses you rendered me during our acquaintance I am enclosing a keepsake. At present value—in your Time—it is worth about two million pounds, so I shall always feel that you can never want throughout the rest of your life. Also I have instructed the lawyers who have handed you this package to transfer my bank account, roughly another two million, to Gregory Vane—not for his personal use but for the furtherance of science. I know he will succeed in founding the Gregory Vane Institute of Science because in my files it is recorded that he will open it in a couple of years.

"Now as to the problem that bothered you—the reason why we could never marry. There were two barriers. One was because I belong to the Future and you to the Present (so-called), which two states can never unite; and also for the much more logical reason that I am related to you.

"In October of next year you will have a son, even as I told you. That son, in turn, will also marry, being a famous engineer when he does so. He will have three children. To cut it short, Glenda, your children will have three children, and in the course of three centuries that can stem out to mean quite a number of people, of whom I myself am one of the descendants! It means that, very remotely, I am a grandson of yours, dozens of times removed. That is why we could never marry, because had such a thing been possible I could not have been born. So you see, as I said, the answer is simpler than you think!

"Goodbye, both of you, and good luck.

Tom."